WRITTEN IN BLOOD

Written in Blood
(Blood Rights, Book Four)

K. B. Thorne

To all the survivors. I see you.

PRELUDE

"My name is Nykk Marlowe." The girl speaking to you is small and skinny. She never meets your eyes. "I guess you already know that. Nykk is spelled with a Y and two Ks. It's not short for Nicole. I know it's a strange name, but it's not my fault. Blame my parents." Stopping, she winces. "That sounds wrong. They aren't... They weren't... They aren't bad people. It's not their fault."

You're patient with her when she stops and looks at something off to her right. Is she listening to something? Does she see something?

It's too soon to ask. After what she's been through, you know you need to let her come to you. You need to give her the chance to come around to it, to everything, on her own.

She's not a very large girl. You guess she couldn't be more than 5'4" or 5'5" and clearly hasn't eaten enough in a while. Her cheeks are slightly sunken, but that's not what draws your eye when you look at her. You try not to stare, but it's hard. The vine-like, angry red scars crawling up the left side of her face are impossible not to look at, even for someone with your training.

"I'm supposed to talk about what happened," she says. She still hasn't met your eye, and there is little emotional affect to her features. Maybe it hurts to move her face too much, with those scars. You make a note of it. "I don't really want to talk about it, but they say I have to. So I guess I will."

Still you say nothing and let her get to it at her own pace.

Briefly, her gaze meets yours. It's haunted. You've seen the look before, but not often like this. "It happened really fast, you know? I barely even remember it, except that it was sudden, and darkness followed. It's like there were two lives, or maybe like there were two of me. There was the Nykk who existed before and then the long moment of darkness before the Nykk that existed after.

"I guess that leaves a frightening question." Her pale brow furrows in the most pronounced show of emotion you've seen yet. "Who am I now?"

CHAPTER ONE

The glare of flashing police lights was blinding.

I didn't need to flash my badge to get through the blockade on I-95 South, because every cop recognized my face. Even if they hadn't met me, everyone had heard about me and the way I look. I wish I could say it's because I look like Jane Russell or Jayne Mansfield, but I'm afraid I'm not that lucky. Even without the calling card of my unique adolescence, I wouldn't have pulled it off.

Driving to the end of the line of cars, I parked and hoofed it to where the party was taking place. I saw that Vance had arrived ahead of me.

"What do we have?" I didn't think it was the time for pleasantries, so I walked right up to where Detective Vance Johnston stood next to the major crimes van, taking notes.

He lifted his eyes to meet mine. "I've only been here a few minutes myself," he replied. "This is going to be on the damned news." He jerked his dark-haired head in the direction of the throttled traffic I'd just barely gotten past using the shoulder of the highway. Turning back to me, red and blue lights glinted eerily off his amber eyes.

I snorted. "Death isn't going to care that a bunch of people desperate to be on their way to the Big Apple are delayed a few hours."

"True." Vance smirked. "Let's go see what we have." He started walking down the short decline of grass and torn-up dirt to a line of skinny trees. "All I know so far is that the victim is a young woman, and the killer was not in a hurry."

My training told me not to make assumptions when I didn't have to, so I didn't think about it. I'd find out soon enough.

Doctor Carl Wright from the Adelheid satellite office of the OCME (Office of the Chief Medical Examiner) was standing a few steps behind Doctor Terrence Cor. Cor was new, so his boss was shadowing him on his first few cases. Around the station, we'd already taken to calling him Doogie Howser. Even if it wasn't quite that extreme, he still seemed ridiculously young to be an MD and working my crime scenes.

The body was surrounded by clear plastic. It looked like she had been wrapped in several layers and taped shut, but it had been cut open; I presume to see what was inside, or the first person knew it was a human being and wanted to see if she was alive. The cut ran from top to middle, revealing a nude teenaged girl. There were bruises patchworking her body in shades from purple to yellow to green-brown, covering the span of time they'd been received. I grimaced.

"Someone did a number on her," Vance commented in a low voice. I knelt on the opposite side of Cor, who was writing things on a clipboard.

Seeing the display of long-term abuse and hearing his particular choice of words set my nerves slightly on edge. There had been a time in my life when I'd looked like that and heard those same words said about me. It wasn't a time I liked to look back at, so I looked at the victim instead.

This girl couldn't have been more than fifteen or sixteen. Her body had been wrapped with her arms straight at her sides. The way the plastic folded around her, but was cut open at the top, made me think of a grisly burrito. An inappropriate comparison, but you can't help what you think. Her head was tilted away from me and her body tilted slightly on the incline, so I couldn't see much of her face, but I could see she had long blonde hair. I gauged her to be average height, but very skinny.

"Do we have anything on her that might give us a clue about who she is?" Vance asked.

"Nothing," Cor replied. "This is all we have. Detritus from the area here will be brought back to the lab, but to be honest, I'm not optimistic that anything will be there."

I sighed. "I'm afraid I'm with you on that one. Any killer that goes through the trouble of wrapping their victim like an obsessive-compulsive Christmas gift won't be disorganized enough to drop their wallet on the way." I glanced back at the unhappy highway. I heard cars honking. "Want to start canvassing and see if we can find all the cars that passed by this afternoon?" I asked with a dry smile.

Vance didn't reply to that. He pointed to her neck. "Strangled?"

Cor nodded. "Looks that way," he agreed. "From the look of the indentations, I'm guessing it was a thick rope. I can even see a few fibers stuck in the wound." He looked up from his clipboard now and met my eyes. There was something in his gaze that I hadn't expected to see, although I couldn't quite identify it. "There's something else you need to see."

I frowned. "What?"

He gestured for me to come around to the other side of the body. I did and knelt when he pointed at her face. It was tilted enough to make it a little hard to make out, but once I did, I felt my blood run cold. Out of the corner of my eye, I saw Vance frown and come nearer. Peering closely, he frowned too.

From below the edge of the plastic, crawling up the side of her body—over her shoulder and up her neck onto her face—were scars. They were red and angry. They were young, as scars went. They weren't just any scars, however. They looked vaguely like vines, like crawling ivy, or where blood had boiled inside one's veins and left an outward mark. They would be described by some like her face had been finger-painted with acid.

How did I know this? The scars running along the side of her body were exactly the same as the ones on *my* body.

"Nykk," Vance began quietly, turning toward me.

I held up my hand. "I don't know how they happened, but I know it's not the same person." I could hear the edge in my voice, but I couldn't seem to smooth it out. "The man who did this to me is dead, and that's the end of the story. This is just a miserable coincidence."

He kept looking at me. "I thought you said that coincidences don't happen."

"Well, it looks like I was wrong, wasn't I?" I knew I snapped and stopped, took a breath, and counted to three. It was unprofessional. I was caught off guard, but I had to put my game face back on. It was the face where the scars didn't matter, and I was able to place them far enough away from me to almost believe they weren't even mine. It took a moment and another deep breath, but I did it. I met Vance's eyes briefly, he nodded in acknowledgement that I'd reined it back in, and we turned to Cor.

"Who found the body?" Vance asked.

An officer in uniform stood off to our left. She was the one to reply. "A woman driving home from work, around quarter to four this afternoon, blew out a tire. She pulled over to the side of the road and got out of the car. When she was calling the tow truck, she saw the plastic and thought it looked suspicious. She got closer and saw the face, panicked and called nine-one-one."

"Is she still here?" I asked. Detective Nykk Marlowe had to be here right now and now she was. I felt better in this skin.

"No, a black-and-white took her down to the station. She was really shaken up and couldn't calm down while still here, but she agreed to go there to make her statement."

"Radio in and make sure she stays there till we get back. We'll want to talk to her." Vance rubbed the back of his neck. I had learned this about him. He did that when some statement or action was just a matter of procedure. We both knew the woman with the flat tire wasn't likely to provide any useful information, but we had to ask anyway.

I watched Cor do his job. "What can you tell us about her?"

He talked while he worked. "She's an adolescent. I'm guessing fifteen to seventeen. She's been dead around eighteen hours, judging from temperature and rigor. I would say lividity shows she was moved after death, but I think that's fairly obvious. I'll know more once we get back to the morgue, of course. She hasn't been here on the road very long."

"How do you know?"

"It rained last night and didn't stop until after ten this morning." He pointed to the plastic. "There's no trace of water anywhere but the bottom of the bag where it is lying against the grass. So, she was left here between ten and three forty-five."

I looked at Vance. "Want to track down everyone who drove this highway during those seven hours?" I smirked without humor.

His expression wasn't any more amused now than before. "We could give it to the media and see if anyone reports seeing anything, but I wouldn't hold my breath." Stepping away to speak with a uniform, I stayed where I was to watch Cor's efforts. He'd be carting the girl off to the morgue soon for an autopsy. While she was still there, I had to look again.

I could feel another version of myself deep inside my head, behind the Game Face, reliving utter, blind terror.

I know it makes me sound crazy, but anyone in a job like mine will know how important it is to set that shit aside. It's like there's two of you. One was watching and listening and thinking like a cop, investigating the crime laid out before me.

The other was looking at this girl, naked and cold and dead, and she was seeing the same height and the same color hair. By themselves, they were details so vague and broad that they fit thousands of women in the state, but with those scars, the *other* couldn't help but see myself in her. I had to remind the other me that this girl was dead and I was alive. The man who hurt me was dead.

Unfortunately, that meant there was another psychopath out there with some skill or ability or poison that was a lot like my guy.

To call it a 'disturbing' thought didn't do it enough justice.

CHAPTER TWO

After a fruitless and short discussion, then dismissal of the woman who'd found the body, a large white board was wheeled into the squad room. We had a printout of a digital photo taken at the scene tacked to the top. I wrote "who is she?" underneath it along with the slim list of pertinent details.

"You should have just written *jack shit*, because that's precisely what we have," Vance muttered. He had his arms crossed across his broad chest, leaning back against my desk and glaring at the board.

I might have replied, but Captain Roy—i.e., our boss—walked in. "What do we have?"

Turning my head from Vance to Roy, I said, "Jack shit, apparently."

Roy didn't seem to find it amusing. Funny, neither did I.

"Teenage girl found wrapped in plastic, dumped off I-95. The wrapping job was thorough, and the body was pretty clean—at least, there was nothing obvious. She was naked with no personal effects anywhere that we could find," Vance began with a quick glare in my direction, perhaps because I'd ratted out his bad joke.

"She's obviously suffered long-term physical abuse. She's covered in bruises of various ages," I continued. Roy was peering closely at the picture. I felt my scars begin to burn, but I ignored them. "She has some unique scarring." I couldn't seem to make my voice reach a normal level when I said that.

The captain apparently noticed and looked at me. Or maybe he was just comparing us. "Did your attacker have an accomplice?" I knew he'd read my file and knew the details of my case.

I shook my head. "If he did, I never had any knowledge of them. No one could ever figure out how this scarring happened anyways, it matched nothing medically known, so there's not really anything to go on." I hoped he'd drop it, because there couldn't be any connection. I knew in my soul that my abductor didn't have an accomplice. Those eleven months of my life were *burned* into every cell.

Roy nodded. "Well, let's try to get an ID on this girl and go from there. Keep me apprised."

"Yes, sir," Vance and I said simultaneously.

We watched Captain Roy go into his office and then turned back to the board. "Let's pull all the files from missing persons for girls in this age range, and make sure the M.E. is doing some prints. We'll see if she's in the system," I said, although my eyes were fixed on the printed photo.

"We'll also run her through the computer and see if there are any other cases with scarring like this," Vance said and then met my eye. "Aside from yours." He paused. "I can't imagine how there could have been without us knowing about it, though." Shaking his head, he started to turn away but stopped and looked at me for a long moment. "Are you okay?"

Damn, I had a bad feeling I was going to be hearing that question a lot now. "I'm fine, Vance. It's just a shitty coincidence."

He nodded and still looked unconvinced. "Do you think there's anything from your experience that might help figure things out for this girl?"

I shook my head slowly. "I don't see how. It has to be a

different guy and since they don't know what did this to me, I can't tell you what sort of people are capable of it."

He hesitated again. It couldn't be easy, asking me questions like this. He probably worried I was going to snap his head off any minute. "Do you remember anything about it that might help?"

"No," I sighed, briefly closing my eyes. "I barely remember the day it happened, and what I do remember is just a blur of burning pain and screaming." I opened my eyes, feeling a flat expression on my face that I hadn't consciously put there, as I turned to him. "It hurt like Hell itself. I don't see how that will help us."

"I suppose not," he agreed with a nod. "I hope you understand that I have to ask."

It was my turn to nod. "I get it, but it's not like I like it."

"Fair enough. I'm going to start working on the computer. Why don't you start on the missing persons files," he suggested and then went to his desk.

I stayed where I was for a few moments longer. I looked at the girl's pale, dead face in the picture. I examined every detail until the pixels the computer and printer had used to make it became clearer to me than the image.

Who are you? She didn't answer. *How did you get those scars?* Silence. I guess she didn't know any better what had happened to her than I had. Still, even if I knew that the similarities had to be passed off as a miserable coincidence, it had to give me something of an edge in finding the truth.

At least, I had to hope so, because otherwise, it just gave me an edge at feeling crazy.

☾O☽

A couple of hours later, I was sitting at my desk with a stack of folders in front of me. We were hardly a big city like New

York or Los Angeles, but we had more than our share of missing people. Too many, I thought as I looked at the stack. There were maybe a dozen and a half fitting into the age and general description I had.

Before I could start examining them more closely, however, my phone rang.

"Marlowe."

It was Cor. "We ran the girl's fingerprints, and she's not in the system." He didn't bother with pleasantries. I was okay with that. "She does, however, have an uncommon birthmark on the back of her right shoulder. It's vaguely shaped like a four-pointed star. I will let you know more once we've started the autopsy."

Sighing, I thanked him and hung up. I had been hoping the prints would give us an ID, but apparently, I was still stuck sifting through paperwork. The birthmark would help at little, though. How many girls that age, body type, and coloring would have a mark like that? (I was hoping not many.)

I opened the first folder. I looked at the picture that had been provided by the girl's father, who she lived with, when he filed the report. She was smiling and happy, and nothing like the corpse on the board. That didn't mean it wasn't her, since living versus dead images can be hard to match. I looked at the date of the report, which said it was filed two weeks ago.

I almost set it aside, because the bruises proved she was getting beat on for longer than two weeks. However, the cop in my brain asserted herself to remind me that this wasn't me or like my case. The bruises could have been from someone other than the person who killed her, so I kept reading.

This girl had a large tattoo of tropical flowers on her lower back. Now I set it aside, because Cor would have mentioned that. And nothing in the file mentioned a birthmark.

Moving onto the next one, I had just gotten to look at one more photo and read about one more parent filing a missing-persons report when my phone rang again. I hoped it was Cor with good news.

It wasn't.

"Detective Marlowe? This is Emily, Emily Miller, down at O'Keefe's?" The voice on the other end of the phone was uncertain. I decided not to point out that I certainly couldn't tell her if she worked at the local supermarket or not, so why did she say it like a question...but my brain had already made the connection. This girl must have worked with my sister, who had a part-time job stocking shelves at O'Keefe's.

"Is there a problem with Ana?" I asked, immediately on edge.

She hesitated but answered before I had to say anything. "I'm afraid so. There seems to have been an argument between her and another employee. The dispute is over, but she's not handling it well, and she won't talk to anyone. We hoped maybe you could get through to her?"

I sighed and put my hand over the mouthpiece, twisting to find Vance still at his desk. "Vance," I called. "Can you handle things here for an hour?"

He frowned. "Sure. What's wrong?"

"Family matter," was all I said before turning back to Emily on the line. "I'll be there in ten minutes." And I was out the door.

O'Keefe's wasn't far from the police station, right in the center of town. It was a local supermarket, so it didn't have the variety of a big chain, but people in Adelheid tended to stick close to home.

Since Cameron's Law had made all preternatural creatures legal and put Adelheid on the map as the center of all things preternatural, a distinctly non-human population has turned small-city living into an art form. Both shifters and vampires have proven to be territorial and thus stay in their territories. And those who've made Adelheid home like the feeling of it and viciously guard it.

There are a few humans who have ended up here, myself and my sister included. I don't know why, but I just feel more comfortable around supernaturals than I do around regular humans.

By the time I had pulled into O'Keefe's parking lot, I already had half a dozen scenarios running through my mind. I had no idea which one I'd encounter.

I walked in and was greeted by Derek Green. He was a werewolf, member of the local pack, and had managed the store for as long as I could remember. I had talked to him a lot when Ana first submitted an application.

"She's in my office," he said and led me to the back of the store where a small office was tucked into a smaller corner.

"Do you know anything else about what happened?" I asked as we walked.

"I don't know what started the argument, but it was between her and Brett, who is another employee with some issues." He always played it cautiously with the labels. I appreciated that. "Apparently, he called her a name, and that's when she started shutting down. She went into my office on her own, shut the door, and wouldn't respond to any of us."

Reaching the door, he opened it for me but let me go in on my own.

On the other side of the room, my twenty-one-year-old sister with Down Syndrome was sitting in the corner with her head bowed. It wasn't the first time I'd seen this happen, but the occasions had been getting fewer.

"Ana," I said, but she didn't respond. Her hair was blonde, like mine, and hanging over her face. I walked over and knelt in front of her. "Ana," I repeated, but she still didn't respond. Reaching out, I touched her chin, and she let me tilt her face up. I glanced at her ear and saw that her hearing aid wasn't in. That explained a lot.

Put your hearing aid in, I signed.

She frowned and looked like she wanted to resist, but her light brown eyes—again, like mine—looked over my expression and realized I wasn't in the mood for rebellion. Putting her hand to her ear, she replaced the piece.

"Thank you." I smiled faintly. "Do you want to tell me what happened?"

"Brett called me a stupid bitch," she told me.

That's just perfect, I thought but didn't say out loud. "He shouldn't have said that. It's not a nice thing to call a person," I assured her. "What did you do when he said that?"

She shrugged weakly. "I told him that was a bad word and came in here. I didn't want him to see me cry." Her bottom lip twitched. "I'm not a stupid bitch, am I?"

"Of course you're not," I said quickly and fervently, leaning forward to hug her. "I think Brett must have just been in a bad mood and said something mean. He shouldn't have said it, though, and just because he did say it doesn't make it true." I leaned my head against hers. "But why didn't you answer to others when they called for you?"

She spoke into my shoulder. "I didn't want to let the others see me cry either. Only babies cry."

"That's not true, Ana. Everyone cries at some time or another." She didn't reply. I held her for a while before asking, "Do you want to go home?" She nodded. "Okay, let's get you out to the car while I talk to Mr. Green for a moment, okay?" She nodded again, and I helped her to her feet, walking with her as far as the door and watching her get into the car.

I turned to find Mr. Greene standing right behind me. "Is this going to be a problem?" I asked, hoping it wouldn't. Finding this job had taken a lot of effort, and it had been working out very well so far.

He considered for a moment, but then he shook his head. "I'm fairly certain that Ana didn't start the fight. Brett has a history of it. So, we'll just let it go and see her for her usual shift tomorrow, all right?"

"Sounds good," I said with relief. "Thank you."

I drove us home but didn't pull into our driveway. Instead, I dropped her off with Mrs. Bauer, our next-door neighbor. A widow whose two children were grown and out of the house, she often stayed with Ana when I was at work. Ana doesn't require a lot of assistance under most circumstances, but neither of us like her to be in the house alone.

After taking care of that, I took a moment in the car to just breathe deep before returning to the office.

CHAPTER THREE

Vance practically tripped me as I walked into the squad room.

"We got it," he announced. He handed me the folder, which I immediately opened and began reading. "Her name is Katerina Scott. She was reported missing last April by Father William, who runs the shelter down on Forrester Street. According to him, she was born to homeless parents and never got into a decent situation. She lost them a year ago and spent a lot of time in the shelter."

The photo clipped at the top showed her amidst a group of others sitting at long tables with plates of food. For the number of mouths, it didn't look like much, but it was probably a lot to them. "Was she into drugs or prostitution to get by?"

Vance shook his head. "Father William said she had managed to stay away from all that."

"That's pretty amazing." I closed the folder. "I wonder what she did, then, that got her dead. Are we going to the shelter?"

"I thought it was the next logical step."

I had been out of the car for all of five minutes and now we were heading right back into it, but this time, he drove. He tolerated my driving when he had to, but like most men, he preferred to be behind the wheel. I made the most of my time in the passenger's seat and read the case file.

Unfortunately, there wasn't a lot. I hoped Father William would be able to tell us more.

Pulling into the Forrester Street Shelter, we found the inside busy. I wasn't surprised. With the economy still struggling, more and more people needed help all the time, and the late months of the year are cold in New England. Even so, Father William was easy to find as the guy dressed all in black milling through the crowds.

We introduced ourselves and got right into things.

"You filed a missing persons report for a sixteen-year-old girl named Katerina Scott?" Vance asked.

The friendly smile that had been on his face began to fade. He nodded slowly. "I did. Have...have you found her?"

I took the digital photo printout and showed it to him. "Is this Ms. Scott?"

Taking the image and adjusting his glasses, his shoulders slumped a moment later and he handed it back. "Yes, that's her." He sighed. "She was such a sweet girl, despite everything she'd been through."

"If you will excuse me for asking," I continued, working to properly phrase my question, though anyone would say tact was not my strong suit, "don't the homeless often drift in and out of areas? How did you know to file the report?"

"It's true, but not Katie," the priest replied with a shake of his head. "She came in for dinner here at the shelter every night, without fail, for the past two years. That's as long as I have been here. When she didn't come in for several nights, I knew something was very wrong."

Vance, better at the tact thing than I was, smiled slightly. "That was a good call," he said. "I wish we had better news for you. Do you mind if we ask you a few questions?"

Father William nodded. "Of course, of course." He ushered us to a quieter corner of the large, open room, and we sat down at a small table. "First, though, please, can you tell me what happened to her?"

"We're not entirely sure yet, sir," Vance said with an apologetic smile. "We do know that she was murdered, but that's why we're here."

He nodded. "What can I tell you that will help?"

This was where I jumped in. "You said she was a sweet girl. Was she well-liked by everyone, or was there anyone she might have been having problems with? It's dangerous for a girl alone on the streets. Did she ever tell you about any trouble?"

"No, if she had any troubles like that, she never said. I know she didn't have any problems with anyone here. Everyone generally liked her, but she didn't really have any friends either. I guess you could say she was a loner, though I suppose it's not much of a surprise. She spent most of her time alone."

I knew what that was like but didn't say anything about it. "Do you know where she spent most of her time when she wasn't here?"

He thought about it, but shook his head. "I'm sorry. This is rather upsetting. She didn't always tell me. I knew she moved around a lot, but never too far from the shelter. She didn't have a car or bus fare, after all."

"Thank you, Father." Vance handed him a card. "If you think of anything, please give us a call. We may be in touch again if we have any further questions."

"Of course," he said as we all stood. He walked us out.

Standing outside, I stuffed my hands into my pockets. The phrase "a damp, drizzly November in my soul" ran through my mind when I looked at the gray sky and felt the chill on my skin. Winters in New England are extreme, harsh things. I didn't envy the people in the shelter behind me, who would spend more time out in this weather than I did. I tried not to think about Katerina Scott, and how she would have been better off in this weather than in the grips of whoever killed her.

"At least we have a name," Vance said as he stood beside me.

"Yeah, that's something," I agreed. It wasn't much, though.

We got in the car and started driving back to the station. I called Mrs. Bauer and checked on Ana. The report was good, which was something of a relief. When I hung up, Vance was looking sideways at me.

"Is everything okay at home?" he asked. "I couldn't help but overhear."

"It's all right." I shrugged. I didn't like bringing too many of my home problems to work, but sometimes, it was unavoidable. "My sister, you met her that once," I waited until he nodded and went on, "she's been having a rough time lately, more outbursts and moments where she shuts down. I'm not sure what's going on."

"I'm sorry to hear that." And he did sound sorry. He was a nice guy like that.

I ran a hand through my hair. I considered telling him all my guilt and insecurity that her emotional issues were my fault, because she didn't get all the early intervention she needed. I didn't, though. "She's had phases like this before and they always pass. I just hope I'm doing enough. It's hard with this job."

He nodded. "It is, but I'm sure you're doing fine. You obviously love her and do what you can to take care of her."

"I try," I agreed.

There didn't seem to be much else to say.

☾○☽

We had just walked through the door when a young woman in uniform, Harper—one of our newest hires—all but jumped in front of us.

"Heads up," she said in a conspiratorial whisper.

Vance and I exchanged frowns before turning them on her. "Why?" I asked. I hoped this was a case of a new officer being over-eager, but I wasn't going to hold my breath of being lucky. Not today.

She bit momentarily on her lip. I couldn't help but think she looked more like a high school sophomore than a cop, but I knew that appearances were deceiving. "The FBI is here."

Oh, that couldn't be good. "Why?" Vance took a step forward before realizing his inner tiger was taking over and forced himself to stop his stalking before it began.

Harper didn't appear to notice. She shrugged. "He didn't tell us peons, but I wanted to warn you before you tripped over him. He's waiting for you in the squad room."

"He?" I frowned. "Is it just one guy?"

"Yeah, though I don't imagine it will stay that way. The feds are like tribbles."

Vance laughed. I frowned at him. The word sounded familiar, but I couldn't place it. He just stared back. "Tribbles… You know? Fuzzy little fast breeders that like to take over space stations and starships?" He waited to see if I was catching on, but I didn't and he sighed. "Do you even own a television? *Star Trek*, for fuck's sake."

I wasn't really sure how best to reply to that. Of course I'd heard of it, but I didn't watch much television. "Whatever." I walked past Harper and just assumed Vance would follow, heading to find this mysterious FBI agent who was undoubtedly coming to complicate our lives.

Walking through the door, I only saw the back of a thick, black head of hair, but the space given him by the rest of the room singled him out. I could see that he was looking at the board for Katerina Scott, and I wondered if she was the reason he was here, but why would the FBI be interested? Perhaps it was just curiosity.

"Excuse me?" I said, walking up to him. "I'm Detective…" My voice died in my throat when he turned to look at me.

I recognized him. It had been fifteen years, but he still looked like he had when we were teenagers. He was a little older now, but his dark eyes and their piercing look were something I had never forgotten.

It took him a moment longer, but recognition dawned in his gaze. Something more complex lingered behind it, though. I wasn't sure what it was.

"Nykk?" he asked, blinking and running his eyes up and down my face. For the first time since I'd been rescued, I wanted to cover my scars. I didn't want this face from the past to see me like that. I kept myself from doing it, but the urge was strong. "Good God, woman. I never knew what happened to you."

"Do you two know each other?" Vance had come up beside us and broke the spell holding me in place.

I turned to him. "Yeah," I said, picking my wits up from where they had dropped on the ground. "This is Jackson Lang. Apparently, Agent Lang now. We knew each other growing up."

Jackson rubbed his head. "We were teenagers together, until Nykk disappeared. I moved with my family to California not long after. I tried to keep in touch with your family, but they had a rough time of it. Eventually, we lost touch, and I never knew… The cops at the time said you probably ran away."

"No." I nearly swallowed the word, watching his gaze linger on my scars. "I didn't run away." I didn't want to talk about this. "It's not really time for Old Home Week. What are you doing here?"

He frowned. A decade and a half later and I could still read him like his face was an open book. He wanted to ask what happened to me and talk about the past. It bothered him to be shuffled off it, but he knew he had a job to do. The thought process ran through his eyes as clearly as words. "Right," he said, blinking. "I'm here because of her." He pointed at the board and Scott's picture.

I looked at her picture and stepped back from him with a sudden urge to hang up the picture from the missing persons file, which had her alive and smiling. "Why?"

"You ran a search about the scars," he explained. "It set off flags for us, because we have two cases."

"What?" Vance and I asked, simultaneously and incredulously.

Jackson picked a folder up off my desk and opened it. He pinned two photos to the board, and the resemblance to Scott's morgue snapshot was eerie. Pointing to each picture as he went on, he said, "Serena Joyce, sixteen, reported missing in February and found in October off I-95 in Waterford." He pointed to the second image, and I realized I recognized that one. "Sandra Clancy, fourteen, reported missing in January and also found in October off I-95, but on the line between Waterford and New London."

Both girls were blonde and crawling with scars.

CHAPTER FOUR

"The FBI became involved because of Clancy," Jackson explained after we had moved to a separate room where we could sit at a table and talk undisturbed. "I'm sure you both are well aware of the case."

"The teenage daughter of a senator goes missing and people notice," Vance said, "and when he's a senator that helped push through Cameron's Law, the preternatural community takes extra notice."

Jackson nodded. "That's right. He wanted heavy hitters, started exerting some pressure, and we were called in from the New London office to assist the case. That's when we discovered Joyce. Her case had originally been passed over. She was a prostitute and was reported by another working girl. When she was found, bruised all to hell, it was assumed that her pimp had somehow done it and set aside. It wasn't until Clancy's body was found that we made the connection."

I sat in silence and just listened and thought. I remembered the news from the previous month about the senator's daughter being found, but there had never been anything about scarring. That would have caught my attention. "How did we not know about this?"

"For once in our lives, we managed to keep something quiet." Jackson smiled wryly. "The family didn't want it all over the media. The press was bad enough. We also wanted to keep some of it to ourselves. I'm sure you understand."

"I'm amazed you got people to sit on it," I muttered,

spinning a pen in a slow circle on the tabletop. "Scott makes three cases. How similar are the cases? Are we looking at a serial?"

Jackson looked at the open file in front of him. "These two cases are pretty close, and you can tell me how well Scott matches up. Both were teenage girls between five-three and five-five with blonde hair and average body types. They were reported missing nine to ten months before they were found. When the body was discovered, it was off I-95, and they were wrapped in plastic. There was evidence of multiple injuries received over a period of months. Both died by hanging." He looked up. "There's more, but the two cases are practically identical."

Vance sighed heavily. "Damn."

"We're still waiting to hear back from the ME," I said, "but so far, it all matches up."

"Then yes, it looks like we are looking at a serial." Jackson's face was mostly expressionless, but none of us liked the statement.

"Damn," I echoed my partner.

As if by magic, my cell phone rang. Wright was on the other line. "I have some results." Not a man of many words, that one.

"We'll be down in a few." I hung up and turned to the boys. "Who wants to take a field trip to the morgue?"

❰❍❱

Wright hadn't even asked who Jackson was. That was pretty standard for him, though, so I didn't bother introducing him either. I knew Wright just didn't care. Cor was there, but it was Wright who did the talking.

"We found multiple wounds in various states of healing. This includes contusions, lacerations, burns, and broken bones. Some of them are just days old while others are months old. The bones look like someone tried to set them, but not very well." He walked around the body as he talked. "The sheer volume suggests that someone intentionally harmed her."

Memories shimmied to the surface of my mind, but I shoved them away with no small amount of mental violence. "Cause of death?"

He pointed to her throat. "She was hanged. Her neck was broken. Someone put a noose of coarse rope around her neck and dropped her off something high. We have fibers from the wound."

"Could it have been suicide?" Vance asked.

"I doubt it. This girl was very undernourished, and her muscles show signs of atrophy. From the scarring and raw spots around her wrists and ankles from rope restraints, I can make the educated guess to say she was kept immobilized for a long period of time."

I swallowed hard. "So she was held hostage and tortured." I got the words out, but they might as well have been acid in my throat.

Wright just nodded. "That's what it looks like." He walked around to her head. "The strange thing, however, is that there is damage to her brain, but like the scars on her left side, I have no idea what caused it. I'm hoping the tox screen will give us a clue, but it'll be a little longer for that."

"Is there any evidence of sexual trauma?" Vance asked.

No, I thought, *there isn't.*

"None that I could find," Wright replied.

Cor stepped forward. "We did find a single hair—short and black—on the body, and it didn't belong to her. We'll run DNA and see if it matches anything already in our system."

I swallowed my thoughts back down. "We have two cases from the FBI that are very similar to this one." I glanced at Jackson. "Would you look at those autopsy reports and see if there are any differences?"

Stepping forward, Cor took the folder from Jackson. "Of course. We'll let you know soon."

"Thank you," Jackson said, and we walked out into the hallway.

My mind raced out ahead of me, trying to delve into a past I didn't want to look at that was staring me in the face. Every time I tried to look away, it followed me like some intangible bully.

We stopped just outside the doors. "I think you may need to talk a little bit more now," Vance said, fixing me with a serious look. "How similar is that to what happened to you?"

I met his look and then Jackson's and back to Vance. "It's very similar," I forced myself to admit. "I was kidnapped and held hostage for eleven months. I was beaten, bruised, and broken until the cops rescued me." Inhaling deeply through my nose, I forced myself to stay calm. "But my abductor was killed during that raid. He pulled a weapon, and two cops fired off rounds. He was dead when he hit the ground. It's all in the reports."

It was only because I'd been told that I knew this. I had never wanted to look up my own case. My abductor was dead. Case closed. Or so I'd thought.

"And as far as I ever knew, he never had an accomplice," I added quickly. "I know how this looks, but I just can't see how it can be connected." I paused. "And without knowing what caused the scarring, we can't presume anything from that. It's like needing to know what kind of bullet before we can find a gun to match to a person."

Vance nodded slowly. "True," he agreed, "but I'm sorry, Nykk, one can't help but wonder."

I rolled my shoulders. The muscles up to my neck were suddenly two-by-fours. "I know, but it really doesn't seem possible. Maybe some psycho read about my case in the paper and tried to replicate it."

"Fifteen years later?" This was the first time Jackson had spoken since we'd come out into the hall. I had almost forgotten he was there.

"It's as good a theory as any," I retorted.

"I suppose so." Vance didn't sound convinced.

Suddenly, I realized it was hard to breathe. I knew it must have been building slowly, because it always happened that way. It built, but I didn't notice until it had its hands around my lungs and was squeezing. Sweat beaded between my shoulder blades, and I felt my heartbeat through my veins. "Well," I said, swallowing hard, "you boys keep theorizing. I'll be right back."

I turned away and headed into the bathroom. I shut the door behind me and leaned against it, pressing the back of my skull against the hard metal. The image in my mind was that I straightened up, making a straight path for the air from my lips to my lungs, and that made it easier.

Was it bullshit? Maybe, but the image and the act had gotten me through an adolescence packed with panic attacks and the decreasing scattering of them through college. I hadn't had one since I graduated, but it returned with a bang. I had the whole nine yards: trouble breathing, pounding heart, cold sweat, the need to flee from everything in sight.

Clinging tight to my mental worry-stone, I forced my breathing to be even and dug my nails into my palms until the stinging points began to draw me away from the irrational waves of fright.

This is not okay, I told myself. If this happened again at the wrong time, it could impact my job, and I couldn't let that happen. I was letting this case get to me, and I couldn't let that happen either. And yet it was hard to escape Vance's point. There were too many similarities to ignore that there had to be some kind of connection, but I couldn't fathom what it was. And it wasn't *my* guy.

I couldn't stand still. I pushed away from the door and paced the length of the bathroom. Whoever had killed these girls was not *my* abductor. If I could remember that, I would be okay. If I could remember that I was still alive and was not fourteen years old again, I would be okay.

That was going to be hard with Jackson Lang outside. He made my earlier life come rushing back into my mind, the memories of *Before* hitting the memories these victims brought up headfirst. I couldn't help but wonder what my life would have been like, if it hadn't been for...

No, I had to stop that.

Turning to the mirror, I looked at myself. I didn't hate what I saw. I had gotten used to it. I was numb to my own appearance. Reaching out, I pressed my hand against the glass and covered the scarred side of my face. I couldn't see it. Now it was just the rest of me. Passably pretty, blonde, pale, light brown eyes. Only a small portion of my body had the scars, but when I pulled back my hand, the angry vine dominated.

I was breathing again, so I went back out and found the boys where I had left them. They glanced up, but I didn't see any clue they suspected anything was amiss, so I jumped right back in where we left off.

FIRST INTERLUDE

"I was late for the bus. It's as simple and as stupid as that." She shifts her hands in her lap, folding one over the other and then reversing them. She stares at them intently, like it's important how her hands are set. You wait. "We were living in an area that had a bus stop for the kids. I was late, and the bus was already on its way. The street was deserted.

"I started to walk back home. I was walking on the grass. I think that muffled the footsteps because I didn't hear him come up behind me." She finally stops fidgeting with her hands and sits perfectly still. "It wasn't until he was breathing on my neck that I knew he was there. I turned around fast, saw his face for a split-second, and then came the darkness. Then came the moment where I stopped being the old me and became the new me."

Her pale fingertips rub at the scars, and she winces in pain again. "Do they hurt?" you ask politely.

Again, her gaze meets yours but only for a moment. "A little, but it's nothing I can't handle. It's nothing compared to..." She trails off and sighs. "I remember having a happy childhood. I'm the oldest, you know, though I've all but forgotten what it's like to be a big sister now. I've had a lifetime of not having been one, you know? I kind of look at my brother and sister now, and I don't know what to do with them." She pauses, and a faint frown creases the corners of her mouth. "Is this what I'm supposed to be talking about?"

You smile encouragingly. "You can talk about anything

you want to."

"Anything I want," she repeats the words distantly. "Except I can't leave."

"No, not yet," you say.

She nods. "I guess I should tell you the rest. That's what they said I had to talk to you about." She pauses again before continuing. "I was still mostly the old me when I woke up, tied to a wooden table in a dark basement, but that wouldn't last long. It's amazing how fast you can change, when someone really tries to change you."

CHAPTER FIVE

Nothing further came in, and we called it a night. I guessed Vance was going to see his vampire girlfriend, since it was after dark and she'd be conscious. I didn't know where Jackson went. He looked like he wanted to talk to me, but I kind of ducked him and headed out.

I picked Ana up from Mrs. Bauer's. She seemed in better spirits.

"Mrs. Bauer is thinking about getting a dog," Ana declared as soon as we had shut the door at our neighbor's and started walking home.

"Is she?" I asked, relieved for something to talk about that wasn't plastic-wrapped bodies beat to hell. "Did she say what kind of dog she was thinking about?"

Ana frowned slightly. "I can't remember what she called it. Was one of those ones without a real face."

I frowned. I knew that wasn't what she was trying to say, and usually I can guess, but I wasn't sure about that one. "I don't think there are any dogs without real faces."

She was quiet, thinking hard as we walked into our house and I turned the deadbolt behind us. "It was one of those that doesn't have a real nose, not a long one like other dogs," she explained carefully as we took off our coats and I hung both up in the closet.

Now, the picture was forming. "Oh, one of the kinds of dogs that have the flat face and usually snorts a lot."

She grinned. "Yeah! One of those. She said they're small and she likes that, 'cause she'd be better able to take care of a little one rather than a big one."

Walking into the kitchen, I sat at our two-person table and began taking off my boots. "That makes sense. A little dog would be easier for her to take care of." I had images of visits with flat-faced dogs in my head now. I just hoped Ana wouldn't want us to get one, too. "What do you want for dinner?"

Lining her sneakers up against the wall, she was quiet for a moment. "Can we have that chicken stuff you made the other night?"

"Sure," I said.

I got the leftovers out of the fridge and warmed them up. We passed a pleasant dinner, and I listened to Ana, who seemed to have forgotten all about the troubles of earlier in the day, chatter on about various things she saw on television or heard Mrs. Bauer talk about. I didn't say much myself, but I enjoyed listening. My hours at work could be rough, so I appreciated the times I could be home to have dinner with my sister, rather than working into the night on the paranormal cases.

And it was nice to be distracted from the day I wanted to leave behind me. It wasn't like it wouldn't be waiting for me on the next one.

While Ana watched television, I got Bunnicula out of his hutch from the back porch. The albino miniature rabbit hopped around on the floor between my legs until taking the piece of lettuce from my hand. Sometimes, I could get lost in watching him and would almost expect him to suck the color from the leaf. My memories of the book were vague, but I remember loving it when I was a kid, before I was taken.

Bunnicula hopped around for a while before settling in next to my leg, eating another piece of lettuce and wrinkling his nose. I liked petting him. It was soothing, almost meditative.

"I'm going to bed," Ana said, getting to her feet.

I looked up. "Did you want me to braid your hair?" She shook her head. "Okay, well, don't forget to brush your teeth."

"I won't." She smiled as I got up and hugged her good night. I listened as she walked down the hall, in and out of the bathroom and into her room. I waited to make sure she didn't call me, or need me for anything. When it was quiet through the house, I turned the television off and carried Bunnicula to the couch.

He watched me for a moment with those strange red eyes, like he was waiting to see if I was settled before he curled up in my lap and wiggled his nose against my hand.

I liked sitting in the quiet. It was strange, because you would think that would make my thoughts worse. It didn't. I liked it. When Ana was awake and the television was playing and the phone might ring and cars drove by on the street, it overwhelmed me, and when I didn't have the job, or Ana's needs, to focus on, that really got to me.

But now she was in bed, and the street was quiet. Mostly humans lived on this street, kind of clumping together in the town and living on the same schedule. There were some preternaturals too, but each breed seemed to stay close. Vampires stayed near other vampires, since they lived only at night. Humans still spent most of their time in the day, except me. Being a cop in Paranormal, USA, meant my hours were hardly predictable, but this street tended to quiet down after dark while the rest of the city came alive.

I didn't want to think about Katerina Scott, or Serena Joyce, or Sandra Clancy. I didn't want to think about fourteen-year-old Nykk Marlowe.

Sitting there, I lost track of time. I let the silence feed my mind so I could vanish into it and not think about the things I didn't want to. Suddenly, it was late, and I realized I should get some sleep. I made myself get up and put Bunnicula back in his hutch, checked his water, and then went to bed.

My sleep was mostly dreamless. In the morning, I figured that was the best I could ask for.

☾○☽

I got into work late in the morning, which was about the usual time. Everything had gone so as-usual that I could almost forget everything that happened the day before, until I pulled into the parking lot and discovered twice as many cars as usual and all with that "we're law enforcement" look to them, yet I didn't recognize a one.

Walking in, I found Vance immediately amid the buzz of activity.

"FBI is stepping in," he said, clearly unhappy about it. His jaw twitched as he watched the feds get their stuff set up. "I suppose we should count our lucky stars they aren't outright taking over."

"Damn." Sighing, I stood beside him. "I had hoped that Jack appearing yesterday meant they were sharing information. I didn't realize he was a bloody scouting party."

Vance shrugged. "That's what you get when a senator presses on the FBI and three girls turn up dead like this."

I frowned. We both knew the truth of it. "Only when one of those girls is a senator's daughter, you mean. Still, I guess maybe having a little extra help won't be a bad thing to catch this guy before he does it again. If we're talking a serial, you know as well as I do that he won't stop until we stop him. Best see if we can do it fast."

"We do, and you know it's the feds that will be taking all the credit."

"If it gets a monster off the street, I can live with that." I looked at him, and he looked back.

"Me, too." He pushed away from the desk. "Come on, let's go meet our new best friends."

Jackson stood in front of our white board with a short woman beside him. I might have mistaken her for a teenager at her size, but she carried the authority of cop. I could see it even from behind. She had the strangest color hair, almost aqua. I was used to being stared at, rather than the one doing the staring.

Hearing us approach, they both turned around. The sight of him still surprised me and tried to pull me into the past, but her eyes drew me. They were large and nearly the same shade as her hair. I couldn't help but think of those anime heroines with the big eyes, tiny noses, and full glimmering hair. Not that I watched it much, but I'd seen enough to get the idea.

Jackson made the introductions. "Detectives Marlowe and Johnston, this is my partner, Special Agent Posey Kai."

Kai smiled, politely but not without warmth, and offered a tiny hand. We both shook it, and I wondered how the hell she had passed the physical requirements for the job. Being only human, I couldn't tell if she was a shifter or something like that. I just knew it was daylight out, so she was no vampire.

"It's a pleasure to meet you." Her voice was smooth, just a few words made me think of those commercials where pouring liquid exchanged places with waving fabric, cultured and educated. "I know this must be very disconcerting for you, to have us in your territory, but we're here to help. I think we can all agree on the importance of this case and getting it solved."

For some reason, I found myself resistant to voicing my agreement, even though I did agree with her.

I forced myself to nod. "I think we can all agree on that." Turning around, I saw Vance was on the phone. I hadn't even heard it ring.

He hung up. "Wright wants to see us."

☾ O ☽

We headed as a group to the morgue. It was strange having my usual team doubled in size, but I supposed I was going to have to get used to it.

Wright and Cor had the three case files open, side by side, on the table when we walked in.

"Well, we brought the party to you, doc," Jackson said as we walked in.

Frowning, Wright looked up and blinked behind his glasses. "What party?"

I could have told Jackson that Wright had no sense of humor, but it didn't really occur to me.

"Nothing. What have you found?" He waved it away.

"The three cases are practically identical," Cor began, "except for the specific injuries, but the general natures are all the same."

Wright nodded. "All three girls are approximately the same age and body type with blonde hair. They were all malnourished and dehydrated, but not enough to kill them. Their bodies all showed evidence of long-term immobility and restraints on their wrists and ankles. They all had signs of old wounds like burns and broken bones that had been inexpertly treated. They also had bruises varying from nearly gone to brand new, but none show any signs of sexual trauma."

Memories flashed behind my eyes. I heard a thin chain rattling as I weakly made a circuit around a wooden table. It was my daily sojourn.

"They were all hanged," Cor went on. "They had a rope put around their neck and were thrown from a high enough place to break their necks. The fibers all belong to a common, coarse kind of rope. They also all had the same unique scarring on the left sides of their faces with no forensic explanation for the cause." His eyes flickered briefly to me, but away again when I met his gaze. "They also had the same brain damage, but the tox screen on these two—" He pointed at the two files furthest to the left. "—came back with nothing that would cause it. There were minute traces of different poisons in their systems, but not enough to kill them and not anything that would damage their brains in that way."

"We can say with certainty that these girls were all killed by the same person," I said, half-question and half-statement.

Wright nodded. "We can say that."

For some reason, that was hard for me to hear. I mean, it was pretty damn obvious they were the same perp, but hearing it was still hard.

"Thank you, Doctor," Vance said.

We stepped out into the hall. I felt something go taut in my chest. "It's time we get well acquainted with Clancy and Joyce," I said.

CHAPTER SIX

Our board now had three faces on it. Every one had my scars. I'd spent sixteen years never seeing another face like mine, but now I had three of them staring down at me.

"Serena Joyce was reported missing by a fellow prostitute back in February and was found in October. The case wasn't given a high priority, given her high-risk profession, and with her body as beaten as it was, they assumed it was her pimp and conveniently overlooked the strange scarring," Jackson said as we sat around the table, pointedly not looking at me as he said it.

Conveniently, indeed, I thought.

"However, her friend—the girl who reported her missing—swore that they worked independently," Posey continued. "Her friend made the ID, but we also matched fingerprints to a prostitution arrest. The case wasn't officially closed, but we don't have anything else."

"Nothing at all?" Vance asked.

The two agents shook their head. Jackson continued, "Reported missing in January and found later in October, we have Sandra Clancy. Daughter of well-known Connecticut senator Joshua Clancy, avid proponent for preternatural rights, even though he's human. On this one, however, we found a fiber on the body. We were able to identify it as a vehicular carpet fiber, consistent with a color used in the 2007 Chevy Malibu. It was a color only used that year."

Kai wrote notes on the board. "We looked up all the

registered owners of this vehicle, and none looked good for killing these girls. But there was one car reported missing since the beginning of 2012—before the first girl went missing—by the owner, Janet Meyers, and it has yet to turn up anywhere. The killer could have taken it and been using it since, but we won't know until we find the car."

"Clancy was last seen getting off the bus. The maid for the Clancy house saw Sandra and said hello before Sandra went to the local convenience store, which she often did. That was the last time anyone saw her. Employees at the store were questioned, but no one saw her. It looks like she never made it."

I sat back in my chair and folded my arms across my chest, looking at the board but finding no answers. "That's what we have?" I asked. "One incredibly unique signature on three victims and a car carpet fiber?"

There was a long pause. "There's also the hair found on Scott's body," Vance pointed out. His posture mirrored mine. "They'll do what they can with that and at least when we catch someone, we'll have something to match."

If, I thought cynically, but I kept it to myself.

"The brain damage is still what draws my attention," Kai said, tapping the board where it was written. "I don't know of anything known to the human world that can do that, so it seems like it would have to be some kind of magic."

"But we don't know anything non-human that does that either," Jackson finished for her.

I inhaled slowly. "I don't remember ever hearing of anything either, so we can rule out the better-known species. We know a lot about vampires and shifters, so we know they can't do something like that. What about the fae or demons? They are incredibly varied, and we know very little about the fae."

Everyone nodded like some giant puppeteer was sitting

above the police station. I couldn't help but think it looked a little ridiculous. Then again, I wasn't exactly at my most settled. A faint haze of unreality seemed to have settled on my life.

"We should talk to some people who know more than us," Vance said.

The cell on Jackson's belt chirped and buzzed. He pulled it off, checked the ID, and excused himself to a quieter corner of the room. The rest of us agreed by silent decision to wait until he was done before we said anything else. We didn't have long to wait, but he didn't look happy.

"The office got a call from Senator Clancy," he told us. "He received a letter claiming responsibility for the death of his daughter as retribution for his efforts to get Cameron's Law passed. They're sending us what they got."

"Is this an anonymous someone or do we have a name?" I asked, tensing.

"No name on the letter, but they got prints. They're running them through the database and will let us know if there's a hit," Jackson said.

We were quiet for a few moments. "What are the chances this is actually our killer?" Vance asked with a mirthless half-smile.

A uniformed officer came over and handed Jackson a few sheets of paper.

"I wouldn't hold my breath," I said. I knew this wasn't going to end that easily, because this case was too deep. Someone didn't do things like this to girls without it running deep, and the perp already showed he was smart. He wasn't going to write a letter and announce his connection, but we'd have to follow the lead anyways.

"That was fast," Jackson commented. "They had a hit on the prints. They belong to a Tim Cagney." He read for a few moments. "He's an activist against the preternatural. He was arrested for altercations during the legality hearings and a rabid follower of Frederick Hughes."

Frederick Hughes had been the poster boy for supernatural hate when Cameron's Law was being worked on. He continued to preach about monsters in our midst long after the law was passed.

"Here's the surprising part," Jackson said. "He isn't known to affiliate with any of the major anti-preternatural groups. He doesn't look like the kind of guy to keep it quiet, so I'm willing to bet he is solo. There are no known ties to LOHAV or PAAS."

Also rising from the slime in the wake of the Preternatural Rights Act were the League of Humans against Vampires and the People's Army against the Supernatural, and while both focused on the same thing, LOHAV was known for its violence. "So he's a basket case that flies solo," I commented.

Jackson looked up from his reading, half-smirking at me before getting back to it. "It looks that way." He changed the page. "Here's the letter: 'Your daughter is paying for your sins in harboring monsters and letting them loose among all our children. Cameron's Law is an abomination. That's why your daughter is dead.'"

"Hell," Vance muttered, "what a thing to receive after learning your child has been brutally murdered."

"I'd say this is enough to bring the bastard in for questioning," I suggested. "What do we know about him?"

Some more pages were shuffled and then Jackson said, "He pays the bills by working at a coffee shop in Niantic and passes his time between sending cruel mail at a studio apartment." He handed the papers to us. "Posey and I will go get him, since we can cover multiple territories. We'll bring him back here."

"To freak central?" I asked, smirking. "Oh, he'll just love

that."

☾○☽

Thirty minutes later found Cagney sitting in our interrogation room. Not more than 5'7", he was skinny with dirty dark hair and sunken eyes. He didn't look like the kind of guy that would kidnap, torture, and murder three young girls, but then maybe that was just because he didn't look like the man who'd abducted and tortured me.

"Did you write this?" Jackson asked, setting the fax copy of the letter on the table.

Vance and I watched from the observation room. We had decided that if we wanted to really unsettle Cagney, we would send Vance in. He carried himself like the cat he was and had those unsettling amber-colored eyes.

Cagney glanced at the letter. "Yeah, I wrote it."

That surprised me.

"You should sign your name to things, if you want to take credit," Jackson commented. If Cagney's admission surprised him, he didn't let it show. "Are you claiming responsibility for the death of Sandra Clancy?"

"Sure I am." Cagney didn't blink or even hesitate.

Vance and I looked at each other. "Did it say anything about psychiatric problems?" I asked. "Whoever killed and dumped those girls doesn't want to be caught, or at least wouldn't give it up this easy."

Inside the interrogation room, Jackson had paused. His expression read 'intense cop stare,' but something told me he was as shocked as we were.

"Are you confessing to murder, Mr. Cagney?" Jackson asked flatly.

Cagney didn't reply right away. Greasy hair fell in front

of his eyes, but he didn't bother to clear it as he folded his arms along the table and leaned forward. "Cameron's Law is an abomination, Agent Lang. Senator Clancy, and the others, deserve to be punished. He's just the first."

Beside me, Vance cleared his throat. I knew him well enough to recognize the sign of agitation. He was always agitated when people started calling his species an abomination. I didn't really blame him.

"That wasn't what I asked," Jackson said calmly.

Cagney smiled. "I prayed for a reckoning," he said. "I *willed* it to happen, and it did. Clancy is just the first."

"Oh, God." Vance snorted.

"Apparently so," I commented dryly. "I didn't know God was a legislator."

"You willed it to happen?" Jackson remained amazingly level. He was good at this. "You willed a fourteen-year-old girl to be taken from her family and cruelly murdered because of her father's political views?"

Cagney sat up straighter, but for the first time, there was uncertainty on his face. "I didn't choose the method. I just prayed for them all to be punished. The method was the work of a higher power."

Kai spoke for the first time. "No higher power had anything to do with this, Mr. Cagney. It was just plain old-fashioned evil." None of us had any way of knowing that the killer was human, but the word got the desired reaction. Cagney frowned. "Why would you think a higher power would scar up the girl's hands like that?"

Cagney shifted in his chair and shrugged. "It's the will of the higher power, not me. I don't know why it would do that, but it did, so there must have been a reason we simply cannot understand." He said it with conviction.

I watched Jackson roll his shoulders. Cagney didn't even know the details of the crime. If it hadn't been obvious before that this wasn't the guy, that did it.

Jackson and Kai left the room. Cagney was scum, but not criminal. He'd be released, since he wasn't under arrest anyway.

"Well, that was useful." Jackson sighed as he stepped into the observation area with Kai right behind him.

"He was telling the truth," she supplied. "He honestly didn't know I was lying about the hands. He doesn't know what happened to her, so he didn't do it. He just thinks some higher power was answering his hateful prayer."

I frowned slightly. "How do you know?" I asked. "Are you a sorcerer?" The term is one of many used to describe humans with paranormal gifts. Some say psychic, but that is often misconstrued for particular abilities.

Her mouth quirked upward in an enigmatic smile. "Of a sort," she replied and would say nothing further on it. "Suffice it to say, I know. He's a miserable human being, but he didn't kill Sandra Clancy or the others."

"There's no charge for being an asshole," Vance said.

I added, "Unfortunately."

CHAPTER SEVEN

We had just walked back into the squad room when someone called, "There's a Father William on the phone looking for Detective Johnston."

He headed straight to take the call while I silently hoped maybe this would mean a lead that wouldn't dead-end in crazy. I wanted this case over with. I wanted whoever was behind it caught and punished, but even more than that, I needed those three dead girls and their scars to stop staring at me.

"Father William was the one who reported Katerina Scott missing, right?" Jackson asked, stepping up beside me.

"Right." I nodded. "We had talked to him just before you showed up yesterday."

"Nice to know my arrival at places is such a pivotal event in a day."

I smiled without much humor. "Whenever the FBI swoops in on a local case, it tends to make waves."

Before Jackson could get in any comeback, Vance rested the phone against his shoulder and looked at us. "Father William says he has a guy down at the shelter who saw Katerina around the time she went missing. I've got a call on the other line I have to take, so can you handle going down there and talking to him?"

My mouth opened, preparing to say "of course," when Jackson's voice came out instead. "I can go with her."

I swung my head around to look at him, but he wasn't looking at me. Vance nodded with a "thanks" before turning right back to the phone, abandoning me with this obnoxious reminder of the past, this Ghost of Christmas That Would Never Be. It was too late and too unprofessional to change my mind, so I followed him silently to the parking lot and into his government-issued black SUV. (Very inconspicuous, that.)

We were already on the highway before either of us said anything. "So, what's your feeling on this case?"

"It's hard to say. Clearly, we're looking at something ritualistic. That must have some kind of importance to the perpetrator, although what it could be, I don't know." I tried to give myself distance between past and present, but it was hard. The pictures on the board flashed through my mind, over and over.

"What do you know about your own case? What was his motivation?" He asked it in a flat tone, obviously trying to be objective but sensitive enough to know I wouldn't like the questions.

I inhaled slowly through my nose. "He was curious." I stared out the window. "He wanted to know how the body worked, how it hurt and how it healed. He didn't tell me much or talk to me much. Even then, I knew he liked the power over me, though. I guess it made him feel...god-like."

"Do you think that's what is going on with this guy?"

"Could be," I replied as impassively as I was able. "The pattern of confinement and injury is similar."

It's identical, Nykk, tell the truth.

"Have you ever looked up your own case?" Jackson asked after a moment.

"No." I inhaled slowly again. "I was rescued, and he was killed. There was no arrest or trial, no mystery, so why look it up?"

He didn't reply right away. "I suppose that makes sense, although I would have wondered about what they found out after it was done."

I shook my head. "I didn't need to know."

Neither of us said anything more until we reached the shelter, but it felt like there was the proverbial elephant riding in the car with us. He wanted to ask more questions, but he couldn't if he couldn't justify the connection to the case. It wasn't his business otherwise. I didn't want to talk about it. This was all bad enough, wasn't it? I didn't need to start a therapy session in the middle of an investigation.

At the shelter, I led the way because I had been there before. Once again, Father William was easy to find. He greeted me with a nod and small smile. The expression said he was being polite, glad to see us but wished it wasn't under such tragic circumstances.

"He's right over here," the father said, leading us to a table toward the back where one man was eating alone during the off-hour between regular meals.

He was a big man, probably 6'4" or more, with bear-like shoulders hunched over his sandwich and bowl of soup. He had a thick beard threaded with gray and dirty clothes, looking like he belonged in the mountains more than the city.

"Vincent?" Father William said, and the big man looked up. His gaze was clear and steady. "These are detectives. They want to know what you told me about Katerina Scott."

Vincent grunted. "Was back in April, weather just getting warm for a while. I knew Kat. She was a good girl." He frowned. "I was passing by the bookstore downtown, looking for a place to sit for a while. I saw Kat there. I saw her there a lot, you know. She liked it there." He paused, catching his train of thought again. "She was talking to a man."

I sat across from him. He looked at me, and I gave him a moment, letting his eyes wander down the red lines from my forehead to my shirt collar. Everyone needed that moment before they could focus. "This was several months ago. Did it stand out in your mind?"

"Yeah," he said. "Kat was really careful about who she talked to, so she didn't usually talk to much of anyone. She had the Father here, and she talked to me. Maybe a couple of the girls at the bookstore, but this weren't anyone I recognized."

"Can you describe him?" Jackson asked from behind me.

Vincent nodded slowly. "He was a short guy, kind of stocky. White. I didn't get too good a look at his face, but he had short black hair." That caught my attention, thinking of the hair we found on Scott's body. "Nice clothes. Wasn't a homeless guy, though not rich-looking either. Middle class, I guess. Just average. Nothing stood out about him, other than he was talking to Kat." Pausing thoughtfully, he added, "Round the middle of April. About April 16. I remember 'cause I got some temporary work around then."

I smiled politely. "Thank you, Vincent." He went back to his food while Jackson and I stepped aside to talk to Father William. "I don't suppose that sounds at all familiar to you," I said.

His look was apologetic. "Do you know how many people I've seen since April? I need more than that to recognize someone." He shook his head mournfully. "I'm not surprised it was the bookstore, though. They're good folk there. They didn't mind Kat sitting in their reading room from time to time."

"She liked to read or just liked the sitting room?" Jackson asked.

"Oh, she loved to read. Her mother taught her how, and she even managed to get a couple of old paperbacks, thriller and mystery type stories, that she carried with her everywhere. Oh dear, those things were falling apart. She'd read those, and sometimes they'd let her read books for sale, even though she couldn't buy them. Good people."

We thanked him for his time and headed out.

"Better than nothing," I said as Jackson started up the SUV. "The short black hair matches what we found on the body."

"It also gives us a time frame. If that was her abductor, she was taken around the sixteenth of April."

We lapsed again into silence as he drove, because a timeframe didn't actually help us right then. After a few minutes, he started talking again. "How's your family?"

The question surprised me, but it shouldn't have. We had been friends as kids and he'd known my family. "My dad died fifteen years ago, and my mom died just after I graduated college. Peter doesn't keep in touch. I think he's in Seattle somewhere, drinking Starbucks and wearing Birkenstocks. Ana lives with me."

"That must be hard," he said sympathetically.

"Which part?" I couldn't help but ask.

Frowning, he shrugged. "All of it, really, but I meant your brother being out of touch and having to take care of your sister. She has Down Syndrome, right?"

I nodded. "Right, but she does very well. She has a part-time job at the local supermarket in town." He hadn't said anything wrong, but I immediately felt defensive. I forced myself to mentally back down. "She has her good days and bad, but she's a good girl." Turning my head, I looked out the window.

"I never said I thought otherwise, Nykk." He sounded a little hurt by my tone, but I didn't comment on that. "Well, you'll have to tell her I said hello."

"I don't know if she'll remember you," I said. "I mean, nothing personal, but she was pretty young at the time."

"True. Well, say hi anyways, and if she doesn't remember me, I won't take it personally."

Some part of me wondered if there was more to that statement than the words that were said. Was he talking about me? I remembered who he was, but wasn't ready to pretend that the last decade and a half hadn't happened and we hadn't been out of touch for all that time. I didn't know what he expected of me, or what would be expected of me in a situation like this. What would other women do? I didn't know.

I didn't know, so I didn't say anything else.

CHAPTER EIGHT

Back at the office, I sat on the edge of my desk and stared at a map that someone had posted on the board in our absence. Last-known locations and body dumpsites were marked off in two different colors. People buzzed around me, working on whatever they worked on, while I stared at the dumpsite markers. It was easier than looking at the pictures of dead girls.

"See anything?" Vance leaned against the desk beside me, crossing his arms over his chest.

"Yeah." I got up and grabbed a pencil, drawing parentheses on the map. "I won't say I want more information because that means more bodies, but there were neither last known locations nor body sites inside this area."

Vance nodded slowly. "It's a pretty big area. Not exactly geographic profiling, but it's a start. We could be looking at the hot-zone where the killer lives."

I nodded. "That's what I thought, though I don't want to get too excited about it just yet."

Jackson and Posey walked into our little circle right then. I told them what I'd just told Vance, but everyone felt the same way. It could be something, but we didn't know yet. And, sadly, probably wouldn't know until there were more bodies. And we all hoped we didn't get there.

The conversation drifted from profiling of the geographic type to the psychological. Apparently, Agent Kai had some behavioral science in her background.

"What do we know about this killer?" she said, standing in front of the board with her arms crossed along her waist. I was briefly distracted by the hue of her hair. "I think we're looking at a male, thirty to forty. He's smart and meticulous, but I don't imagine he's in a challenging profession. Might even be, to him, a demeaning one."

"Isn't this what all serial profiles say?" Vance asked. "I mean, I didn't get the training, but I could come up with the same thing."

She glanced at him over a slender shoulder with a dry smile, but without any apparent irritation for his tone. "Maybe, but that doesn't mean it's not true. We're just talking about statistics here." Turning back to the board, she pointed at the various items. "What do we see here that isn't like the others?"

"His mother was blonde," Vance said. This case was bothering him. The sarcasm came out more when he was bothered. Like all men, he used humor to cover up emotion.

"I won't rule it out, but I doubt it," Posey replied, sounding distracted and thoughtful. She held up one hand, fingers moving like they were slowly playing an invisible musical instrument. "They're all young, around the same age, and I'm sure that has significance. The source of what drives him. They were all kidnapped, held for long periods of time, tortured, then killed. No sexual assault."

Vance cleared his throat. "It doesn't even look like there's that element to the injuries. They don't look ritualistic, but more systemic."

Sitting on the desk to my right, Jackson nodded. "I'd agree. He sets the bones, like he is taking care of them, but then does all this. He's got a purpose, and I don't think it's just to maim them."

"When he's done, he executes them." This was from me, and I kind of surprised myself by saying it in the first place. It had been an errant thought, really, but it just popped out.

Posey turned and looked at me. For a moment, it felt like she was evaluating me for something, but I didn't know what. I met her gaze and held it, trying to reveal as little as possible in mine, but I still got the uncomfortable feeling she could see deeper than I wanted her to. I waited for her to say something.

"That's a good insight," she finally said. "Although they are malnourished, dehydrated, and injured in more ways than any body should be, they don't die from this. He keeps them alive, and then chooses when to kill them. Is it the power of it, or is he simply done with them?"

"He's just done with them." Words came unbidden again. I willed my mouth to stop talking without being sure of what it said. I didn't want to say too much that would give me away. We needed to remain focused.

Posey was still looking at me. "What makes you think so?"

I shrugged. "Right now, it's just a feeling."

She looked at me for another long moment and then nodded, turning once again to the board. I was relieved when she did. Although having the Ghost of What Might Have Been sitting beside me was bad enough, her gaze was remarkably unsettling. I knew I should have been talking more about what had happened to me, even if it was just a place to start theories about this guy, but I didn't want to. It wasn't the same guy, so why should I have to dredge up my own issues any more than I already had? Could it really help at all?

"Like I said, he's smart," she continued.

"Look at the way he's wrapped them up. There's been just barely more than jack shit—" I got a dry look from Vance here. "—for physical evidence with the bodies. They're clean and wrapped carefully, like the world's most grotesque Christmas presents. He knows what he's doing."

Jackson pointed at the map. "And the dumpsites are

chosen with care. Plus, who the hell pays attention to cars on the side of the road when it's a busy one like 95? That was clearly no mistake."

Whatever was going to be said next was interrupted when the door to the captain's office opened and Captain Roy poked his head out. "Marlowe, in my office?"

"What did you do this time?" Vance quipped with a half-smile, although there was concern in his eyes, too.

"Woke up this morning." I pushed off the desk and walked into Roy's office, not wanting to keep my boss waiting.

Although not a tall man, Roy was broad and seemed to fill up most of the space behind his desk with his barrel chest. Leaning against the shelf behind him with his arms folded, he didn't look angry, but he didn't look happy either.

"Yes, Captain?" I asked, not sitting down or asking if I could. I just wanted to know what was going on.

"How's the case going?" he asked after a long pause.

He didn't call me in here just to ask me that, I knew. Still, I couldn't say that, so I answered his question. "Slow, I'm afraid. It looks pretty clear we're dealing with a serial, which is going to make our job more difficult. We have very little physical evidence or eyewitness accounts. Right now, we're discussing the psychological aspect and geographic profiling, of a sort." True geographic profiling was a little more scientific and exact than just staring at a map and drawing with marker.

"Anything from the letter the senator's office sent over?" he asked. I told him about our interview. "Keep me up to date. The senator is not happy, and once the public catches wind of this, neither will they be."

"Yes, sir." I nodded slowly. He wasn't saying anything I didn't already know, so I waited patiently through his pause, waiting for him to get to the point.

Finally, he did. "Detective Marlowe," he said slowly,

staring at his desk for a long moment. "You know I try to stay out of the personal lives of my officers, unless there's reason to worry it'll impact their jobs."

I saw where this was going. He met my eyes.

"Although there's no conclusive evidence linking the two, there are similarities between your case and these girls that we can't ignore. I would be remiss in my duty both to the case and to you if I didn't ask, can you handle this?" He paused briefly before adding, "There's no shame in stepping off this one. Although I know it tastes bad, having the FBI here means we got plenty of help."

Out of respect for the gravity of the situation, I didn't give a knee-jerk reply. I held his gaze while I thought it through.

The truth was that I had my doubts. Anyone would. But I also knew there was no way in hell I could step off this case. I had to know what had happened to these girls, and I had to be a part of it. I had to help, and I couldn't help from behind a desk.

I nodded slowly. "I can handle it, sir."

He eyed me for several more moments in stony silence, like he was evaluating what I said and trying to read into it, look deeper into me. Whatever he was looking for, he didn't find. Or did find. I didn't know what it was, but he was apparently satisfied because he nodded.

"Then go figure out who is doing this before there's another dead girl," he said and waved me out of his office.

I managed a quick "thank you, sir" but didn't linger.

Chapter Nine

Leaving Roy's office, I did my best to not look or feel like a kid who had just been let out of the principal's office. I kept my head up and my face impassive, reminding myself inwardly that I was a grown woman and this had just been a quick chat with my boss; that he wasn't doubting my capabilities, but that anyone in my situation would need to take a good look at things before deciding to proceed.

Everyone was pretty much in the same place I'd left them, except for Vance, who was closer to the door. Sadie, his vampire girlfriend, was there, and they were leaning close to one another. It didn't look romantic, but like they were having a conversation they didn't want anyone else to hear. With their supernatural hearing, they could talk too low for my poor human ears to ever pick up so I wasn't sure why they were so worried.

For a moment, my eyes lingered. I knew it was rude, but I couldn't help myself. I wasn't quite myself since this all had begun, and talking with Roy had gotten it a little more stirred up. Issues I usually kept stuffed deep drifted upward.

What would it be like to be...*normal*? Funny how I was looking at a vampire and a weretiger having a conversation and thinking of them as 'normal,' but there it was. It was the two of them, in a relationship, like normal adults— normal adults who went through an average childhood and adolescence and weren't strapped to a wooden table in a dark basement for eleven months during the most formative period of their lives.

I wondered if I'd ever get to know what that was like.

Now I was being stupid. I shook my head and turned back to where Jackson and Kai were standing in front of the whiteboard, pointing at lists in marker and talking animatedly. I sat on the edge of a desk and looked things over myself.

"Is everything alright?"

Vance's voice to my right startled me, but I didn't let it show. I turned to look at him, glancing over his shoulder. Sadie was gone. They were quick, vampires were, I'd always have to give them that. I looked at him again. "Sure, everything's fine," I replied, thinking it was only slightly a lie. "Roy was just checking in with me."

He nodded slowly. "Checking in on the case or on you?" He was a good cop, no doubt, but I couldn't say I was thrilled to have him turning the investigation beam on me.

I smiled faintly. "Me," I replied, "but it's all right. It was a fair question. I said I could handle it and he said okay, so I'm still here."

"Good," Vance said without hesitation. "I'm not sure we can crack it without you."

"It's not the same guy." I was getting tired of saying that...and wondering each time I did if it was true.

He shrugged. "I know, but you're still going to know more than the rest of us, Nykk. Come on, let's see what the big kids are talking about up there."

Jackson turned toward us first as we approached. Neither of them said anything about my having to step away and dove right into it. "We were still discussing the psychology," Kai said. Her voice still made me think she wasn't meant to be in this line of work, but perhaps talking about rare and expensive antiques in New York City or singing somewhere elegant. "Although television has turned it into something of a pop psychology concept, it doesn't make it less worthy of note." She turned back to the board and pointed at the picture of Sandra Clancy. "This was the first girl to be taken, and unless there are earlier victims we have yet to find, this makes her the first. There could be meaning in that. She could have a personal connection to our killer."

As far as I knew, I was the only person ever taken by the man who'd kidnapped me, and there'd been no connection there. I didn't say it, though. She had already acknowledged it was a possibility rather than a given.

"What do we know about Sandra Clancy?" Vance asked, grabbing the file. Jackson had one of his own.

They began with what we already knew about her age and parents. "Her friends said she was an outgoing, friendly girl. She was a solid B student and well-liked by her teachers. No one knew of any problems she had with anyone. She liked English and drama. She liked to read." He turned a page. "Mysteries and thrillers, apparently. More than one friend repeated jokes she had made about having the last name Clancy."

"Mysteries?" I asked, feeling a chord strike in my mind. "Our homeless girl liked to read those, too." I shuffled papers to find that file, flipping through reports. "According to the priest at the shelter, she had two that she took with her everywhere, and the local bookstore let her sit and read without purchase."

"It's probably just a coincidence," Vance said thoughtfully.

"Probably, but it's worth noting." I closed the file. I tried to think if we could make anything more of it, but nothing came to me.

Kai sighed. "If this weren't a serial, I'd say we needed to look at the senator more closely, because in Sandra's case, he's the most obvious source of trouble."

"He's only a lightning rod because of his support of Cameron's Law," Vance pointed out. "If all these girls were killed in retribution for that, wouldn't they be preternatural?"

We all considered it.

"That would depend on what's going on in the head of our psycho," I said. "If he's punishing Senator Clancy, he may target humans to do just that: I'll kill your people. Clancy is human, after all." I shook my head. "This doesn't feel like a crime of revenge, though. I'm with Agent Kai. If it was just the daughter then maybe, but not with all of them."

No one seemed able to disagree with that, for the moment, and that brought our thought circle about Sandra Clancy to an end. We turned to Scott and Joyce, who were harder because they had been so isolated. Scott was homeless and Joyce had been a prostitute.

"When was the last time Joyce's family heard from her?" Vance asked.

"Three years ago, when she ran away from home at thirteen. Her family lives in southern New Hampshire and apparently never worked that hard to find her." Jackson's tone made it clear he didn't think much of that.

I looked at her picture on the board. "Who was the girl that reported her missing?"

Back into the file. "Tina Carter, another working girl. They took her statement but didn't work too hard on it."

I rolled my eyes and then turned to Vance. "I think we should talk to her again."

"I agree." He looked at the FBI. "Mind if we take this one?"

Jackson waved at the door. "Be our guest," he said. "We're going to stick around here and wait on the boxes of hate mail from the senator. It might be a dead end, but I want every road mapped."

Giving him a waving salute-like gesture as he led me out of the room, Vance replied, "Sounds like a plan to me."

SECOND INTERLUDE

"*I didn't recognize the room as anywhere I'd been before, but I knew I was in a basement. It was a small basement. There was just the table I was on and a table off to the side with all sorts of things on it. I couldn't see them very well from where I lay, but I would later learn what kinds of things were kept there.*" Here she pauses, closing her eyes against some invisible pain as she takes a shaky breath.

"*Do you need a moment?*" you ask considerately.

She takes another shuddering breath but shakes her head. "*I'm all right.*" She opens her eyes. The pain has fled and is again replaced by the flat look. "*I could smell bread baking, faintly, through the tiny window. It was cracked open just a little, but I couldn't see or hear anything beyond it. I didn't scream, because I didn't think anyone would hear me and I was afraid of who had kidnapped me. It's strange how your mind attaches memories to something like a smell, isn't it?*" Her flat expression shows hints of curiosity then sadness. "*But it does. I struggle with the smell of baking bread.*

"*When I woke, I felt strange. I must have been drugged.*" She sighs and looks off into nowhere again. "*He came to me that night and told me to call him Master. He didn't touch me that night.*" Pausing, she turns back to you. "*He never touched me in...that way, the ways of men and women. Sometimes I wish he had and then had just let me go, but it wasn't that.*

"*It was worse than that.*" There is a brief moment where her face crumbles inward, like her memories are a hand that *just closed around the paper of her face, but then she shudders once and catches herself, regaining her control. "I don't know his name, because I've never asked. I don't want to know. I just know that he was very strange. He talked to himself a lot. At first, I always thought he was speaking to me, but he wasn't."*

She brushes a hand through her hair. "He liked my hair. He said that a lot. And sometimes when I was thrashing or crying, suffering through whatever he had done, he would stroke my through it." She shakes her head. "So strange."

CHAPTER TEN

We left the station and headed onto the highway to go to Waterford, where Serena Joyce had lived and worked for the past three years. We were silent for a little while, both locked into our own thoughts. I didn't know what Vance had on his mind, but I knew there was plenty on mine.

When the silence was broken, it was Vance that did it. "So, ever gonna share the story about you and Agent Lang?"

That was both unexpected and not. I shrugged. "There's not much to tell. We knew each other while we were growing up. We were friends." In truth, we had been a little more than friends, but we had still been young then. "But I got abducted and was kept for a long time. I haven't heard from him since."

"That's too bad," he said. It wasn't in his nature to push, unless he was on a case, of course. But this would be more in the category of gossip than detective work. Though that wasn't a fair statement, since I knew he wasn't asking to pry but as a friend and a good guy.

We didn't say much else until we got to town, but unfortunately, our information about Tina Carter was pretty slim. There was no home address, but there was a note about where she usually worked. So we started there, but it was a cold drizzly night, so there weren't many girls out working, and none of them was Tina Carter. None of them seemed to know her, either, or at least none admitted it.

Striking out there, we next went to a diner she was reported to hang out at, but that was a dead end too.

"I don't know about you, but I'm feeling exceedingly lucky," I commented dryly as we drove to the Waterford PD. "I want to smack the officer who took this initial statement upside the head."

"Let me do it," Vance said. "I'm a shifter. It'll hurt more."

I chuckled. "That's not a very good attitude for a police detective."

Turning into the parking lot, he looked in my direction. "I won't tell if you won't."

We got out of the car and headed inside. I got the usual double-takes as I walked in, but I ignored them.

"We're from Adelheid PD," I introduced us and we flashed the badges, proving we were all on the same team.

"What can I do for you?" the kid in uniform asked. I couldn't imagine he'd been out of the academy more than five minutes and thus there probably wasn't much he could do, but I didn't say it.

"We're hoping you guys could do us a favor." Vance stepped in. "We're looking for a young woman in the area, works as a prostitute. Her name is Tina Carter." He began to give more information, but a woman in uniform happened to be walking behind us right about then.

She stopped. "You guys looking for Sweet Tina?"

We turned to look at her. "I guess so," Vance said. "Do you know where she is?"

"Yeah, she's in the tank right now."

Vance and I exchanged a look. That was one hell of a piece of luck, and the third time really was the charm. We turned back to her. "What's she in for?" I asked, just to be sure, although we could guess.

The officer shrugged. "Solicitation, nothing new." Her wisdom imparted, she moved on and we got directions. Vance immediately went off to find someone with a modicum of power, and I went to the lock-up.

There was only one person inside at that time, so it was pretty easy to guess who it was. She was a little thing, probably sixteen or seventeen. Hispanic, with long black hair in a messy ponytail and the outfit one would expect. She was leaning back against the bars with her eyes closed. A girl this age should have been in a pink bedroom somewhere, talking on her smartphone, not sitting in a grim cell.

"Tina Carter?" I asked.

Her eyes opened and she looked at me, frowning as her gaze roamed over my face. "Who wants to know?"

I showed my badge. "I'm from Adelheid."

The frown faded. "Oh, that would explain it then." She looked away. I didn't bother to ask or explain. "What do you want? I've got no business in that town."

"I want to ask you some questions about your friend, Serena Joyce."

That brought her attention back around fast. "Nobody's been interested in her. I tried to tell them we were independent, but they said it was the pimp she didn't have and that was that. What're you here for, then?"

Vance showed up with yet another uniform. "It's good to have friends," he told me and then turned to her, making the same obvious assumption I had. "Ms. Carter, I've gotten you set free on the basis that you agree to help us."

She jumped to her feet. "Sure," she said. "Whatever you want."

The officer unlocked the door, and we walked out of the police station. It must have been a nice change of pace for her, I thought. "We can talk in the car and bring you home," I suggested.

"Sure," she repeated and gave us an address. We all piled in, and Vance started driving. I turned around in my seat to face her.

"We have new evidence about what happened to

Serena," I explained plainly, although I didn't plan to give away the store. "I can't tell you much, but we're looking at her case fresh from the beginning. So, tell us everything you remember."

Pulling her jacket around herself, she nodded eagerly and licked her lips. She looked out the window. "Was a while ago now," she began. "She went missing back in February, you know. She was a nice girl. You don't really meet a lot of them out here."

"How long did you know her?" Vance asked kindly.

"Almost since she got to the area," Tina replied. "She was pretty skittish at first, 'cause things were pretty fucked up at home, you know how it is. She liked to read, which is something else you don't see a lot out here."

That caught my attention. "Did she like to go to bookstores?" I asked, thinking of Katerina Scott.

Tina shook her head. "Library," she said, "and usually to find the newest Patterson novels when they came out, which is like one a week these days, isn't it? Even I've noticed." She laughed, but it was kind of mirthless. "Anyways, you want to know about when she disappeared. Okay, I don't remember the date. This was almost a year ago, and my memory isn't that good. I remember what happened and what I tried to tell the cops."

"Okay," Vance encouraged.

"We had been out together that night and were just walking along. It was slow, and there weren't many people out. It's fucking cold in February in this state. We realized, though, that someone was following us. We thought maybe it was a job, but the car never pulled up. I thought maybe they just wanted one. Usually more than one being there doesn't stop anyone, but first time for everything. Serena decided to head home 'cause she was tired, but I stayed out. I kept walking down the street, thinking maybe the car would come after me while Serena split off down a side street. I walked a little ways and turned to wait."

"What happened then?" I prompted.

"The car followed her. I guess they wanted a white chick." Tina shrugged and then looked really sad. "I didn't know..." She trailed off.

Vance jumped in. "There was no way you could have."

I gave her a moment before asking, "Did you get a look at the driver?"

Tina shook her head and sighed, shoulders sagging. "All I saw was a shadowy outline, but he had short spiky hair, messy but like it was supposed to be that way, that rolled out of bed kind of style."

"What about the car?"

She bit her lip and looked up thoughtfully. "I saw the Chevy logo on the front, but I don't know cars too well. It was dark, like black or dark blue, and it wasn't a new car but it wasn't super old either."

That was apparently all we were going to get, so we dropped her off at the address she'd given us and drove back to Adelheid.

"It wasn't a crime of convenience," I said as we cruised down the highway. "Tina would have been the easier mark. He wanted Joyce."

We batted ideas around, but nothing stuck. None felt like much good, so we just got back to the station, reported what we'd found, wrote some notes on the board, and decided to call it a night. Vance said he had a date, and Kai just headed out. Jackson waited for me and walked with me to my car.

"Frustrating case," he commented quietly.

"Yeah, it is." How could one argue with that, after all?

He looked at me for a moment before asking, "Are you doing okay?"

I returned the look while I tried to decide if it was a

casual question, or if he had seen something that made him worried. I didn't think I'd let anything slip, or that anything had come up to make one doubt me...but it was hard to be sure. I didn't know how I seemed from the outside, not for sure.

"Of course," I replied as flatly as I could, still holding his gaze, although those eyes hadn't changed one bit since we were kids and I wanted to look away. But cops don't flinch. "I've got to get home for my sister, though. I'll see you tomorrow."

Getting into my car, I pulled out of the parking lot and didn't look back.

Chapter Eleven

It was late enough when I got home that I left Ana at Mrs. Bauer's. She'd be asleep by then, and I didn't want to wake her up just to go home and go back to bed. I owed Mrs. Bauer a lot, working hours like this, but she genuinely seemed to enjoy Ana's company.

This meant the house was quiet as I walked in, and I didn't mind. I could use a little quiet at that point.

I made myself something to eat and then got Bunnicula from his hutch. Once he was settled in my lap, I got out my phone and dialed Dr. Kohl in New Hampshire. It was late, but I knew she'd be awake. Even though she was human, she'd begun keeping vampire hours and found her business to be booming. You'd be surprised how many vampires started seeking out psychological counseling once they could talk about their real history without being locked up for it.

"Kohl," she answered.

"It's Nykk," I replied. "Are you busy?"

"Not at present." Her voice was always warm. "I haven't heard from you in a while. I hope everything is okay?"

Dr. Kohl was my second therapist. I had been dumped immediately into counseling after being rescued, but I'd changed doctors after a while. Something to do with our health insurance, but it was okay, because Kohl had been wonderful. When I moved out of the state, she said I could still call whenever I needed her.

"It is, I think," I said. "I don't know, to tell you the truth. There's this case I'm working on. I can't tell you much about it, obviously, but it's more than one dead girl and there are some similarities to me. But they're dead. It's been really hard to keep us separated, you know?"

"Yes, I can understand how that would be difficult." I could see her leaning back in her chair, phone to her ear and legs crossed. Her toe would shift from left to right when she was listening intently or deep in thought. "Do you think you're managing to do that?"

I knew I couldn't answer too off-the-cuff with her. She'd catch me, so I paused and thought it through. "I think so, but I guess it's hard to be sure. I think it's getting a little easier as the initial shock has worn off, but I never expected to have this happen. The details that are similar are pretty surprising. It's made my coworkers ask more than once about the man who kidnapped me, but he's dead. I know he is."

"And you've told them that?"

"Of course," I replied. "They believe me. It's all in the reports. But still, it's been weird." I paused. "It doesn't help that there are some others involved. It's become a joint case." Again, I didn't want to give too many details. "One of the people who has become involved is someone I knew when I was a teenager. Do you remember me talking about Jackson Lang?"

She paused. "Yes, I do recall. He was your childhood sweetheart before you were abducted, right?"

I sighed wistfully, leaning back into the couch cushions and stroking Bunnicula's fur with my free hand while he chewed on my pants. "Yeah," I said softly. "He was my first kiss. Just a couple of days before I got grabbed. That kind of makes it stand out, you know? His family moved to California while I was missing, and he didn't even know what had happened to me till he showed up in the middle of this case."

"How do you feel about working with him?"

"Okay, I guess." I became a lot more uncertain when talking with her, I decided, hearing all the 'I guess' and 'I think' phrases coming out of my mouth. That's what one gets when talking to a therapist, I supposed. "It makes it harder to keep the past separated from what I'm working on, though. He keeps reminding me of it, just by standing there."

Knowing me too well after all these years, she asked, "Are you talking to him at all, or are you avoiding him?"

I grimaced. "I can't avoid him entirely. We're working together."

The pause that followed told me my answer had not impressed her. "You know that's not an answer to my question, Nykk."

"I'm avoiding him."

"You shouldn't do that," she went on, though not sternly. "By isolating him, you're preserving him as an image from the past. If you talk to him and get to know him now, you'll be able to get to know him as the present day Jackson rather than the Jackson of sixteen years ago. That should help you separate the two."

She made a good point. She always made good points. It was why I kept calling her. I just couldn't imagine forging a relationship with a new therapist like I had with her.

"I'll try," I conceded. Even if it was a good point, it didn't mean her advice was always easy to follow. "It's harder to separate from the cases, though. I can't talk to them."

I could picture her smiling sympathetically. "True, and without knowing more about them—which I won't ask—I can't offer as much advice there, but you obviously are aware of the issue and are consciously working to combat the problem. That's the biggest step to staying ahead of this." She paused, and I heard a buzz. "I've got a client here for an appointment. Are you going to be all right?"

I smiled a little. "Yeah, I'll be all right. Thanks for talking to me, Dr. Kohl. Do I owe you anything for this?"

"Not this time," she replied kindly, "but you should make an appointment for a phone session soon and let us have a real talk, okay? Take care of yourself, Nykk, and you know my number if you need me."

We hung up, and I did feel a little bit better.

❪O❫

I got Ana from Mrs. Bauer's the next morning, and we had breakfast together. She helped me clean the house before I brought her to work. I ran some errands and then headed into the station.

Unlike the previous days, it was remarkably banal. The senator's office had delivered three cartons of his hate mail, which we spent the day combing through and sorting into piles. We worked to dig up some information on the ones in the "suspicious" pile, but to no useful end.

I tried talking to Jackson throughout the day, but it was as hard as I'd expected. Still, it was a start, I kept telling myself. What was also hard, though, was the feeling of everyone looking at me sideways. I told myself I was being paranoid and I was sure that I was, but that didn't lessen the feeling that every time it got quiet and someone looked at those pictures, they immediately looked at me. Scars were examined and contrasted and compared. The two of us being weighed and measured and considered.

Perhaps I was being unfair to the coworkers around me. If any were looking at me any differently, it was undoubtedly just concern for my sanity and maybe they weren't wrong, but I didn't like it. I didn't like being the center of attention, and I'd felt that way since we found Katerina Scott off I-95.

It was a relief when the day was over, even though it wasn't a relief we'd not found out anything new.

CHAPTER TWELVE

That night, I had a nightmare.

It was dark, nearly pitch-black but for a sliver of light coming from above. I couldn't move, but I wasn't tied down. There was only the manacle around my ankle, but I knew Master didn't like me to walk around during the night. He could hear the chain rattling against the wooden table leg when I did and would tell me to stop.

But I was awake. I couldn't sleep. Whatever he'd given me before leaving made my insides burn. I squirmed against the wooden table and heard my thin dress tear as it caught against a thick splinter. I whimpered and forced myself to stop moving.

Trembling, I wiggled my fingers and tried to think of anything to distract me from the pain. It hurt so bad I wanted to scream. I wanted to scream, but I wasn't allowed, and I couldn't disobey. I wanted to scream, and...

...I woke with a gasp, a strangled inhalation with my hands slapped over my mouth before I was even fully conscious.

The bedside light was on. It was always on while I was in the room. It was dim, but it gave me enough light to see where I was. I told myself I was stronger than this and forced myself to pull my hands down. I was in my bedroom. I made myself look slowly around and take in each wall of my well-kept, comfortably decorated bedroom.

I looked at the pale blue armchair in the corner. It was

my dad's. I remembered him sitting in it on Sunday mornings. He would call me Nykky and tell me stories while I sat on the floor, looking up at him, with a stuffed purple rabbit named Bubbles in my lap, and now Bubbles sat in the chair.

Silver framed pictures lined the top of the dresser, reflecting in the mirror. I had pictures of my now dead parents and my AWOL brother, but I liked the ones of me and Ana the best. I liked the one of me and her when we were younger and before I was different. Even with Ana's problems, life seemed a lot easier then.

The tightness in my chest began to loosen, and I began to breathe easier. After a few minutes of looking at my room, comfortable and warm, I was able to get rid of the chill and lay back down. The sheet was still damp with sweat and a phantom pain lanced through my ankle, but I was able to relax enough to feel drowsy again. And soon, I was able to fall back asleep.

The next morning, I got up with Ana and made breakfast for her. I felt my middle of the night panic attack weighing on me, but I pushed it aside. I couldn't afford to think about it too much.

I poked at scrambled eggs and visualized eating them, though it didn't help me get them in my mouth. After a moment, I was aware of Ana staring at me. I looked up and met her gaze.

I loved my sister's face. I know she looked 'strange' to other people, looking like the typical Down Syndrome face, but I always thought she looked sweet, and there was no concealment or subterfuge in her gaze. She was always open and honest, which was something I clung to when I got home from work sometimes. It was something I needed very badly after a long day in a job full of lies and pain.

"What is it, Ana?" I asked, forcing a weak smile.

"What's wrong?" The question was simple, but I wasn't sure how to answer. I asked what she meant instead. "You aren't you. You're different lately."

I suppose I couldn't argue with that. I thought I'd been doing a better job of hiding it from her, but apparently not. Putting down my fork, I sat back in my chair. I wasn't sure how much I should tell her. She didn't know much about what had happened to me, because it just hadn't seemed right to tell her. But as such, how could she understand what was going on now? And it wasn't like I could tell her much about the case anyways.

"It's just something at work, hon," I said, shaking my head. "I can't really tell you anything. It's just been kind of hard, but I'm okay."

"Really?" she asked.

I forced a better smile. "Really."

She seemed to believe me, because she nodded and went back to eating breakfast, and I began to eat too, in an effort to look like I was feeling okay.

After we finished, we both showered and dressed. I took Ana to work and then took care of some things before heading into the station around midday.

Vance nearly clotheslined me as I walked into the squad room. "You're just in time," he said. The words might have seemed flippant, but his tone and expression were anything but. "There's another body."

My stomach dropped into the soles of my feet. I didn't have to ask him if he was sure. Instead, I nodded and followed him out to the car.

"Lang and Kai will meet us there."

"Where are we going?"

"She was found off I-95 again. This time, it was in Niantic. The local cops will be there, but the FBI has already pulled jurisdiction for us."

In any other case, it would be a surprise that the FBI would let us remain. I wondered if it had something to do with Jackson and me, but it seemed unfair to presume he was letting personal feelings influence his professionalism.

There wasn't much else to say until we got there. Wright and Cor were working with the body while Jackson talked to them and Kai was speaking with some uniforms. It was the same chaos of sound and lights that the last closed-down highway scene had been.

"Teenage girl, blonde, emaciated, bruised, strangled, scarred, wrapped up in plastic," Cor said, looking up as we neared.

"We'll need the autopsy to confirm all of the details," Wright said blandly, writing things down on the omnipresent clipboard. "But I don't think it's unreasonable to say it's the work of the same killer."

Looking down at the girl's face, seeing 'those' scars, I thought it was pretty damn obvious it was the same killer. There couldn't be two of them running around at the same time. There just couldn't.

Frowning, I looked away from the body and saw some technicians making prints of the dirt. My brows rose, and I turned to Jackson. "Are there tire tracks?"

He smiled mirthlessly. "Yep, and the proximity and positioning with the body make it a good guess they belonged to the killer, or at least the car that transported the body. They'll get those back to the lab and see what they can do, but the technicians think from looking at the prints already made that they have enough marks in the tread to possibly ID the tires, if we find the car."

"That's something," I said. "It's more than we had before."

He nodded significantly. There wasn't much to go on here, after all, so we had to hold on to whatever we could. "It looks like she was killed between twelve and eighteen hours ago, but there was a D.O.T. clean-up crew doing this area of the road at eight this morning, and obviously the body wasn't here, so she was dumped somewhere in the past four hours."

Somewhere in my mind, it felt like the killer was getting a little messier than he had been before, which was something to take note of.

☾ O ☽

There hadn't been much else for us to accomplish at the scene, so we headed back to the station. After finding Scott's body, we had already pulled the missing persons files of the gender and ages we needed, so it was easy to dive back into them. Vance and I sat at a table with the stack of files between us.

Now there were four. It disturbed me more than I wanted to admit.

"I think I got it," I said, flipping through pages and then holding up a photograph that looked like a school picture. The face looked like hers, though it could be hard for us to tell between the living and the dead. "Crystal Davidson, a high school junior reported missing in May. She lived with her mother, Anne Marie Davidson, who was the one to file the report." I handed the file to Vance, and he looked through it, nodding.

"Looks like her," he sighed. "All right, let's get the mother in here."

It didn't take long to get the mother on the phone, like she had been waiting beside it for six months. She probably had. Vance fielded the call, but from listening to his half, I figured out how it went, and we headed down to the morgue. Davidson had left work immediately to come down and look at the body.

They did it through a window. I didn't know if it helped or not, but it's what it was. Jackson was there, and I let him and Vance handle it. I would have melted into the walls if I could've.

Anne Marie Davidson was a short, curvy woman with dark hair. She kept wringing her hands in a way that reminded me of my mother. I tried to keep my face averted. Instinctively, I thought seeing my face after seeing the girl's would be difficult for her, and more so if this was indeed her daughter.

Vance stood at her side and walked with her to the window. The curtain pulled back and revealed the girl's face. Davidson made no noise, but she began to sink to her knees. Jackson and Vance both moved quickly to catch her before she hit the tile, and they helped her to a seat. Vance knelt in front of her while she cried.

How did he do it? It was always him. I had never been good with this part. Vance always seemed to know the right words to say, when to keep distance or when to hold a hand or pat a shoulder. I'd seen him hug people before, it was rare but it had happened with particularly emotional cases. Jackson looked like he was the same way.

I was the one standing on the outside. If I could have had the shadow-melting skills of the fae, I would have sunk back into the shade of the corner and not come out again until there was a bad guy to chase.

After a while, it seemed like forever, the mother calmed down. Vance nodded for me to come over. I approached in time to hear Vance ask, "Can we ask you a few questions about your daughter?"

The woman licked her lips anxiously, but she nodded. "She was a good girl. She got good grades in school, didn't get into any trouble. I worried she kept too much to herself." She trailed off and smiled sadly. "Maybe now I wish she had kept more to herself." She looked at her hands in her lap. "She, uh, read a lot and spent time on the computer. She liked to write fanfiction from television shows and books. Let me read some of it, though I didn't understand a lot."

Vance smiled kindly along with her. Jackson reappeared without my having noticed he'd gone and gave her a cup of water, which she took and sipped slowly. Her attention remained on Vance, the source of her comfort. I was glad she hadn't noticed me yet. "We live very close to the school, so she walked unless the weather was bad, but it was May, almost the end of the year. But she never made it. I don't get home till four, and she wasn't there. She was a good girl, you know? She always left me a note or called or sent me a text, and she hadn't. They think she was taken right off the street." She took a deep breath and shuddered. "It's a busy road, but there's...there's a blind section they think she was grabbed from."

I wondered if the cops had pursued the angle that the girl had run away or worked a straight kidnapping idea. We would check the notes at the time the report was taken, but now we knew. "That would suggest she was being followed. He may even have known her routine," I said, still keeping my head averted to try to keep her from seeing my scars if she did look at me. "Did she mention having trouble with anyone?"

"No, never," Anne Marie said with a quick shake of her head. "I think she would have told me. She was a good girl."

"I'm sure she was," Vance said. "May we come take a look at her room and see if there's anything that would give us a hint there? You said she spent a lot of time on the computer, perhaps we could take that and look at it?"

A look flashed through the woman's eyes that I had seen in others—resistance at the idea of their child's privacy being violated—but then came the realization that it didn't matter now and was, in fact, necessary. Dropping her head, she nodded.

"Thank you, Mrs. Davidson," Jackson said. "An officer will take you home."

She got to her feet, walking carefully with the paper cup of water still clutched in her hands. Pausing in the doorway, she looked back at us, her eyes falling again on the source of her comfort. "Please find out who did this to my baby," she said softly and then left.

Chapter Thirteen

We all took a break long enough to get food, but everyone brought it back to the office and ate while we worked.

After Crystal Davidson's mother had left, we hung around long enough to talk to Wright and Cor. The autopsy on Davidson was priority, but the initial inspection looked just like we thought it did. We expected all of the same results. Between that and getting food, we were back at the station about the same time as some uniforms came in with items from the Davidson house.

Nothing stood out, but Kai fired up the computer and began looking through the hard drive while the rest of us looked at the board with its new list of information and its new picture. Its new lifeless, scarred face stared at me with closed eyes.

We had our map marked off with the suspected kidnapping places and dump sites, and I stared at the dots like a pointillism painting. "No girl was left near where she was taken," I said thoughtfully. "I don't know if it means anything else, but it means this guy is planning things. I think the distances are too pronounced to be random, or even subconscious. I think he picks his places ahead of time."

"Given the meticulous nature of everything else, it's safe to say that if this aspect *wasn't* planned, it would be a shock," Jackson said.

Vance pointed at the parentheses I'd drawn on the map. "Davidson still fits into your idea of a potential hot zone, even narrows it a little."

Sighing, I shook my head. "Not enough," I said. "We're still looking at a big area."

We all stared in thought for a while. "There's something about the time line that is bothering me," Vance moved on after a moment. "We have girls taken in January, February, April and May…but then they're dumped inside a few weeks, a couple of months."

"He's cleaning house," I said, feeling something go flat inside. It shouldn't have affected me that way, given what we knew already, but it did anyways. "He's been keeping these girls simultaneously, doing different things, but whatever it is he's been doing, he's done. He's killing them and getting rid of them, carefully and systematically."

"But what has he been doing?" Jackson asked. The confusion in his voice was shared by all of us. "What is this grand scheme that requires kidnapping and torturing teenaged girls?"

A phone on the desk behind him rang, and he answered it. He listened for a little while, thanked the person on the other end, and hung up. "Do you remember the fiber? I had the lab see if the tires could be consistent with those on a 2007 Chevy Malibu, and it's confirmed. Guess it doesn't help us much, but it's a start."

Kai walked over to us. "Unfortunately, Crystal's computer isn't giving us much. I found mostly homework assignments. She had an e-reader library stuffed with books, a few seasons of television shows, and then the usual email and chat programs. The girl was not secretive. You could log right into everything. Mostly emails to friends, some with family and teachers, and a few fan letters to authors she liked, and then the fanfiction." She smiled ruefully. "*Castle* and *Numb3rs*. She had a thing for Colby Granger."

I hated it when that happened. A three-dimensional picture began to coalesce of the victim. It was inevitable.

When someone was killed and you dug into their life, you got to know them. Sometimes, it just hit you harder than others. Something about Crystal Davidson touched a nerve.

Things hit a lull then. Jackson and Kai went off to their own corner, undoubtedly to talk about FBI business us little local cops couldn't be privy to. I decided to go down to the basement, where a gym had been set up. It wasn't much, of course, because we weren't the highest of budgets around, but it did the job. There was a weight machine, a heavy bag, pull-up bar, and sparring mat. Everything was also triple reinforced, because some of our officers were supernatural and were a lot stronger than humans.

I changed and went straight to the heavy bag. I eyed it while I taped my hands, noting a new patch of duct tape. I was guessing one of my previously mentioned preternatural comrades had a go at it and got a little too hard. Luckily, it wasn't at any risk from me.

I liked to kick, and I liked to keep moving. The bag thudded and swung with my strikes, which increased in furor as I kept going. The more I hit, the clearer my mind became. My knuckles and legs began to get sore, but I liked the pain. Sweat trickled down my face, over my scars, it clustered around the vines of tissue that roped its way from my face over my chest and down to my hip. I blinked moisture out of my eyes and kept hitting until I was out of breath, my heart pounding hard, and I leaned against the bag.

I breathed deeply. I focused on it. I knew whoever had taken those girls was not my guy, but I still wondered. What would have happened if the cops hadn't found me and saved me? Would I have been killed and dumped? Images of hanging from a coarse rope thrown over the side of a house flashed before my eyes, but I pushed them aside because I couldn't afford them.

There were four girls counting on me. Only I could help them, because I understood what they had gone through.

The others would try, but none of them would be able to know what the scars on their faces and the scars on their hearts had been like. But they were dead, and I was alive. And I was their chance.

Drying myself off with a towel, I was getting ready for a shower when Vance appeared at the bottom of the stairs. "Nykk," he shouted. "Wright's on the phone, and he's got news."

Forgoing the shower, for the moment, I jogged up the stairs behind him and into the squad room. Vance turned on the speaker phone.

"Go ahead, Wright," he said.

"Cor is finishing up the autopsy," he began, "but we discovered during a more in-depth visual inspection that the victim was not naturally blonde. She dyed her hair. It's clear she was in captivity for several months, but the bleaching was kept up. Not well, but maintained."

For some reason, my gaze met Kai's over this news and we shared a significant look, although I wasn't entirely sure what each of us was saying.

That sunk in for a moment before Vance prompted, "You said you had something else for us?"

There was another pause, and I pictured Wright blinking owlishly. "Oh, yes, we heard back from the lab about that hair found on Scott's body." There was another pause and the sound of keys tapping on a keyboard. "It belongs to a female, and not the victim."

It was remarkable how what amounted to two hairs could shake everything up.

"Are you sure?" I asked.

"Of course," Wright replied, sounding almost offended that we would question him.

Another significant look was quickly passed around. Vance thanked Wright and hung up. No one seemed to know what to say right away.

"We had assumed the killer was male," Jackson said quietly.

"They almost always are," Kai replied. "Statistically speaking, serial killers are male, and female cases are rare. They happen, but they're rare."

I gripped my shoulder, trying to squeeze the tension from it. "This changes everything." I sighed. "What did that homeless guy say about the man he'd seen talking to Katerina Scott?" I thought back. "He only saw him from behind. He said the man was short and kind of thick with short, spiky black hair. Tina Carter said something similar about the driver following Serena Joyce. That's a rather androgynous description."

Jackson snapped and went to grab a folder. "There was a car matching the make and model that had been reported stolen. The owner was female, so we didn't think much of it..." He found the sheet he was looking for. "Let's find out more about her."

"Good idea," Vance agreed.

My nerves buzzed. "I'm going to take a quick shower before diving back into this."

CHAPTER FOURTEEN

I took a lukewarm shower and got dressed in a spare set of clothes I kept in my locker. I had struggled to think of nothing while showering, which meant I had thought of everything. Any nerves that had started to calm down from my vigorous workout were electrified again, and I didn't think I'd ever get them to ease up. I wasn't sure I'd ever be okay again.

When I got back into the squad room, the normally beehive-like atmosphere was quiet while people gathered around a television set. Frowning, I knew that nothing good could come of this and walked up to the crowd.

"What's going on?" I asked.

Vance jerked his head at the set. "Senator Clancy is holding a press briefing." His tone was flat.

When the victim's families began to speak to the press, it rarely meant anything helpful for us. When that family was a famous politician's? It was going to be worse. I kind of didn't want to watch, but I forced myself to stay with the crowd and hear what the man had to say. It wasn't that I was unsympathetic to his pain, but his grief was probably going to make our job harder.

"Weeks after the discovery of my daughter's body and there is nothing," he said, shoulders bent as he leaned against his podium. Anger and resignation warred in his tone and posture. "If the police were better at their jobs, my daughter and these other girls could have been saved.

Held and tortured for months before being killed, there were many wasted opportunities."

"I like it when people start knowing our jobs better than we do," Vance muttered darkly. "Does he think the cops in their areas didn't *want* to find the girls?"

Kai smiled sympathetically at my partner. "He's hurting," she said. "He doesn't know who to be angry at. We're easy targets."

Vance grunted.

"Why are they dragging their feet? Why has there not been justice brought for our daughters?" Clancy went on. "Why was it allowed that our girls should be tortured, evidence of their agony written in terrible scars on their faces?"

"Shit," I muttered.

We had been keeping that detail to ourselves, and now the senator had just 'outed' us on television. Everyone else was mumbling and cursing as well. We had wanted that information to use against the suspect, to help determine the real perpetrator, and because we never thought the voyeuristic public needed *all* the grisly details.

The senator was still talking, but many of us had stopped listening. I pinched the bridge of my nose as I felt a headache coming on, pounding at my temples and behind my eyes.

"Son of a bitch!" Jackson suddenly snapped, slapping his palm against the top of a desk.

My eyes opened, and I looked at the desk, seeing a scorched handprint. Everyone went silent and looked at him with surprise, except Kai. I looked from the burnt wood to his hand and saw it glowing red, but he closed it into a fist and the glow vanished.

Pyrokinetic.

I had never known, but then, sorcerers only came

forward since the legalization, and I hadn't known him then. Still, it was a shock.

"Sorry," he murmured and then left the squad room. Kai looked at us and then followed him.

My eyes trailed after him, but I tried to stop myself from thinking about it. We didn't have the time. "We need to get a hold of the senator and ask him nicely if he'll back off," I said flatly, without looking away from where Jackson had gone.

Vance was beside me. "I've already got people on the phone trying to reach some of his staff, but no one is getting through. We'll try more after he's left the podium, but I doubt he's going to want to talk to us right now. Maybe we'll send someone over to him if he won't pick up his phone."

We were quiet for a while, minds churning. Finally, I had a light bulb go off over my head, and I turned to him. "What about Sadie?"

Frowning, he looked like he was about to ask "what about her?" but then he didn't, because his own light bulb went off. "Good idea," he said instead. "Get your coat." And we were off, stopping just long enough to tell the feds where we were going.

In addition to being a vampire and Vance's girlfriend, Sadie Stanton ran what was becoming a well-known and well-off business devoted to helping the preternatural communities and helping the human populace *with* the preternatural communities. She offered consulting services herself, plus she had an animator, a summoner and lawyer, and a hunter all on the payroll. Considered fair-minded, she was respected in Adelheid and had been an asset on more than one occasion, despite some of her own troubles some months ago.

But while all that was good, it wasn't the reason I suggested we talked to her. One of the reasons she had begun her business and gotten the reputation was because she had been a very public face during the legality hearings that led to Cameron's Law becoming reality. She had been one of the first—as I understood it, she wasn't *the* first but was the second—supernatural being to come forward and admit to the world what she was. All things considered, it was a really ballsy thing to do. While I'd had my head-butting moments with her in the past, I would never deny I respected her for that.

Because of this, though, she knew Senator Clancy. She would have worked with him a great deal during that time and might still have an "inside" line to him now. And being she wasn't the police, she'd probably have a better chance of getting him to talk to her and maybe even to listen.

We didn't say much during the drive. What was there to say? We had four dead girls and a lack of clues that would have been laughable if it wasn't so tragic.

I had to hope that something would turn up with the information we had learned today. My brain hadn't had time to fully process some of it, like the hair. We assumed the hair being on the body meant it belonged to the perpetrator, and it almost certainly did. But it also belonged to a woman. A woman had done this? It was hard to comprehend. Not that it was beyond the comprehension of any cop that women could be just as evil as men, but this kind of crime was almost always committed by men, hence the original profile.

This changed everything. Maybe the clue about the car would turn something up. We had more now than we had before, and we knew it was not laziness or apathy on our parts that had kept us from saving those girls or from finding their killer.

I didn't want to admit it, but Clancy had touched a nerve. I already knew that separating my story from these girls was difficult and maybe even impossible, but what he'd said about missing the opportunity to rescue them hit too deep, because I had been rescued. Though in my case, it wasn't anything the cops could have figured out themselves but just that moment of happenstance—the event that could not be predicted—but why had I been lucky? I had gone through hell, but I was alive to tell the tale now, so what made me different? Why did I live and these other girls die?

The car coming to a stop in front of the Stanton Agency jerked me gratefully out of my thoughts.

We got out of the car and walked in. I planned to let Vance do all the talking, but I wanted to be here to know what she said. As we got through the door, I saw Sadie sitting on the edge of Madison's desk—Madison being the night secretary, and Sadie's roommate and best friend. They were looking at a small television set in the corner of the front office.

Sadie looked at us as the door clicked shut and smiled slightly. "I saw," she said, cutting down our need to explain the situation.

Vance smiled gratefully. He probably wanted to go to her, hug or kiss or do whatever 'normal' couples did, but I appreciated his discretion. "We were wondering if you still had any contact with him."

"Not much since Cameron's Law was signed," she replied, sliding off the desk and walking across the room to turn the television off. "I called him after Sandra went missing and again after her body was found, express my sympathy."

"Do you think he'd take your call now?" he asked. I recognized the signs of tension in his body, and who could be surprised? We didn't need someone leaking information, especially someone with so much public focus, and we didn't need the public turning against us. This was hard enough as it was. "Do you think he'd listen to you? Give us room?"

She inhaled deeply, and I wondered why. She was a vampire and thus didn't need to breathe, except to talk, but I knew she wasn't even a full century old yet—though getting close. Maybe old habits died hard.

"I'm more than willing to try," she said after a few moments, but her shrug was uninspiring, "but I don't know that he'll listen. He's not an unreasonable man. He has always been incredibly just and level-headed, but no father can be either when their child has been killed. He's grieving and he's angry and he's helpless."

"We know, Sadie," Vance said with a weak smile.

"We're not unsympathetic to that," I added, strangely compelled to add my voice to the conversation now, "but we do need to talk to him and hopefully get him to listen."

She nodded and sighed. "I'll see what I can do."

Third Interlude

Unable to sit still any longer, she pushes herself to her feet. Before she walks, she looks at you. "Is this all right?"

"Of course," you answer without hesitation. If she is more comfortable standing or walking, you are certainly not going to tell her she can't.

"I don't like being still for too long," she says. "I can't stand it."

You nod. "I can understand that."

She laughs. It's more like a bark and is an unpleasant sound. "I doubt that," she replies before shaking her head. "He was curious. He had a terrible curiosity. I can't explain it all any other way. He did things to me just to see what would happen. I was his own personal medical school cadaver, who just hadn't had the good grace to die yet."

Absently rubbing her bony wrists, she starts pacing behind the chair she had been sitting in. "He bruised me and broke bones and burned me and cut me and poisoned me, just to see what would happen. He told me this was what he was doing. He didn't tell me why he wanted to know. He just wanted to know."

You listen. She's stopped talking for a moment, thinking about things you can't imagine, or don't think you want to try imagining.

"If the cops found anything to show why he was so curious, they never told me. I haven't asked either." Her fingers

move from her wrists to her face. "I don't know what did this. I know it hurt worse than anything else he did to me, even the burns and the broken bones." That laugh returns. "The doctors in the hospital, where I was taken after I was rescued, said it was a miracle. He actually took care of me after, set the bones properly so they all still work right."

She closes her eyes. "A miracle."

CHAPTER FIFTEEN

While Sadie went into her office to make the call, Vance and I stuck around to see how it went. Madison—a sweet-natured werewolf who was more like a little sister to Sadie than anything—was nice enough to get us cups of coffee, though I wondered if caffeine was what either of us needed right then. She got back to work, and we were left to our own devices.

After thirty minutes had gone by, I was hoping that was a good sign. Though lost in my own thoughts, I was getting kind of antsy and beginning to wonder if our time wouldn't be better served back at the station if this was going to take much longer.

The front door opened, and a man walked in. I had never seen him before, but the ease at which he blew through gave me the idea that he was an employee rather than a client. He was tall and lean, with light brown skin that made me think of a mixed racial heritage and light brown hair. Without apparently noticing us, he went straight to Madison's desk, and they talked in office code for a few moments.

When he turned around, he finally saw us and stopped short. He had startlingly green eyes to be set in that skin tone, and it really made them stand out, but as much as his eyes drew mine, I drew his. He didn't say anything, just stared. I was used to this happening, but only for a couple of moments. Most people had the good grace to look away and pretend they hadn't been staring when we both damn well knew they had.

I didn't say anything. He didn't say anything.

After several moments too long, I felt Vance bristle beside me. "Donovan, man, what's the deal?" he asked roughly. He obviously knew this guy, which strengthened the idea that he was more than a client, and I felt briefly warmed by Vance's defense of me.

"I'm sorry," the man—Donovan, apparently—said with a sharp shake of his head, scratching his scalp. "I didn't mean to stare, really, but I've never seen someone demon-touched like you."

The room had been quiet before, but a new level of silence descended inside of it and inside of my head. Some small switch flipped, and I stopped blinking. I might have even stopped breathing for a moment, feeling things get colder. *Demon-touched?*

"Say what?" As questions from both adult and police detective go, it wasn't my best, and I was generally good at interrogations.

"Donovan O'Malley is the agency summoner," Vance explained. "He summons demons from other planes of existence for a living."

"What do you mean, demon-touched?" I repeated my question with a little more intelligence.

The lanky man folded himself to a seat on the edge of the coffee table. "You guys probably don't know a lot about it, but some demons leave marks. People with these marks are called demon-touched."

I shook my head. "A demon didn't do this to me," I said, for some reason struggling to believe the idea that it had been. "A human man did this to me, a now dead man."

Donovan shook his head. "I know what I'm talking about, Detective. Nothing of Earth can do that a person."

Vance looked between us. "Let's go somewhere and

talk."

☾ O ☽

That 'somewhere' ended up being Donovan's office, which was an interesting room. It didn't look like any office I'd ever seen, with no primary furniture of any kind and a big circle of white writing on the floor. There were scorch marks in the center of it and on a couple of walls as well.

In other circumstances, I probably would have spent more time looking. I'd never seen a summoner's work before...or so I thought.

"Would you please explain for the ignorant what you're talking about?" Vance asked. There were a few folding chairs in the corner that Donovan set up for the three of us, and we all sat down.

"I studied about this while training with Master Anthony," he began. "He was one of the few I've known who'd met someone himself. We use the term 'demon' in my work to describe multiple types of beings. My work deals with beings from alternate planes, which are not demons in the standard religious sense of the word. They are not evil. But there is a class of demons that are evil. We don't summon them, but we learn about them."

"Are you saying it's one of those types that did this?" I asked, trying to not be impatient. I wanted him to get to the point. Did the hell I went through have something to do with a demon? And, if so, what bearing did that have on our cases now? I had to know, and he wasn't getting to the point fast enough.

He nodded. "In this classification, there is a very rare sub-class. They are incorporeal demons who used to be human."

"That's possible?"

"You've got to be kidding me."

Vance and I spoke at the same time. Donovan didn't look at all surprised by our shock and just nodded knowingly. "Like I said," he began, "it's very rare. Only certain demons can do it, and it's only possible with certain people. The demon possesses the body and then they merge. When the physical body dies, the human soul lives on as part of the demon." He paused. "This demon can't possess entirely of its own will, though. It has to be summoned by someone who wants to deal with evil."

The word 'evil' rang in my head like a gong. Of course, that had always been said about the man who kidnapped me, the one who made me call him Master, but it still struck a resounding chord deep within, something I couldn't entirely define the effects of.

"What do you think caused your scars?" Donovan asked, meeting my gaze. Those shocking eyes in that deep tan face, standing out so much, were unnerving. Or maybe it was the conversation. Or both.

"They never had any idea," I replied, almost like an automaton. "But so many different things had been done to me, things that were human and mundane though still damaging, that they could never be sure. They thought maybe some kind of poison. It was sixteen years ago, long before Cameron's Law. They never would've had anything else to think it was."

Donovan nodded. "But now we know these things."

Vance sighed next to me. "You say this is very rare? A demon that would leave a mark like this?"

"It takes someone being able to call on this demon, and then the pair being able to merge. It's rare that it happens. And for some reason, these merged demons are compelled to mark their victims with their individual...signature. We summoners are trained to recognize the signs of the mark. But yeah, it's really rare." Again, he looked at me. "You're the first I've ever met."

Vance went on, "Well, then, this is a day for the record books. The guy who hurt Nykk is dead, but we got four dead girls with scars just like hers right now."

I watched the summoner's green eyes widen. "God," he said, pressing his fingers to the center of his forehead and briefly closing those eyes. Opening them again, he shook his head. "I'm not sure what else I can tell you. There are some drawings I saw while still a student, but I've no experience at all, and I'm not sure any summoner in the area does. It's *that* rare." He sighed thoughtfully. I guess the shock of our news made him repeat himself. "I can look into our archives, though," he added.

My brows knit. "You guys have archives?"

He looked briefly offended but shook it off fast. "We have a central location for the region in Hartford. It's a work-in-progress, really. We've always had summoner circles, even when we used to have to hide them, but records and information were scattered between them. Now we can organize, and we chose a place in Hartford to keep our books and scrolls and writings. I can get access to it and see if there's anything in there about this type of demon. I'm not sure what would be of any use, but I can try."

"Any information would be good," Vance said.

"But there's probably no way to use it to actually find this demon, if that's what it is," I said, feeling pessimistic.

Donovan shook his head. "Not precisely. It won't be, like, a GPS to where this demon is, but there might be clues about locations they'd want to be around. For example, some demons need to be near water. Others will only inhabit certain types of people. It's not much, but if there is something, then I'll let you know." He frowned. I realized he looked really young, and I wondered just what his age was. "Four dead girls? God." He shook his head again. We hadn't told him much, but apparently the idea of murdered girls was enough to unsettle him. It was a decent thing, I thought.

Vance looked at me, and I met his gaze. It took me a moment to realize what was going on in his head. He was wondering how much we should tell Donovan. If he had more information, then he might be able to find more for us. But these were open investigations, and Donovan was a civilian. It was a delicate line.

After a moment, and without any help from me, the decision seemed to be made, and he turned back to the young summoner. "Thanks for any help you can give us," he said. We all got to our feet and headed back to the front office.

We found Sadie waiting for us.

"Did you get through?" I asked, wanting to think about something else, some other angle, for even just a few minutes.

"The senator didn't want to talk to anyone," she said with an apologetic smile and shake of her head, "but his wife actually took my call. She didn't have much to offer that we don't already know. He's hurting and doesn't know what to do. She can't tie him to a chair, but she'll try to see if she can curb any more thoughts of press conferences."

"I suppose that's the best we can hope for right now," Vance sighed.

Sadie put her hand briefly on his arm. "I'll try again later and if I make any progress, I'll let you know."

He smiled at her, and I looked away. "Thanks," I heard him say.

Although we had gotten more information than we'd expected, I was grateful when we left.

Chapter Sixteen

When we got back to the station, both Jackson and Kai nearly tackled us when we walked through the door. Naturally, they wanted to know if we'd talked to the senator and we relayed that, but then quickly ushered them into a room where we could tell them the other part of what we found. I let Vance do most the talking.

As expected, Jackson and Kai were both looking at me when he had finished, and I knew they were seeing my scars in a new light. I suddenly felt like I had as a teenager, wanting to pull my hair over my face and perpetually look off to the left so that side of my face was hidden. I resisted the urge on both counts, but it was a struggle. It even went so far as tightness and a twitch in the muscles of my neck.

"I suppose it's a theory that's as good as any other," Kai said. Her tone was slightly uncertain, but the lilting quality to everything she said made you not care about that. "According to Mr. O'Malley, then, our killer would have somehow summoned this demon and been possessed by it?"

"That's the general idea," I said flatly, still resisting old instincts. "This demon would have once been human." I don't know why I felt compelled to add that, since it didn't help us right then.

"Did he say what happens to the demon if the human host is killed?" Jackson asked. His question struck too close to home, to something I'd been thinking of myself.

Vance shook his head. "I haven't worked with many

summoners or demons, but I think I gather that the demon will be expelled from the corpse and float around in some demonic purgatory until it's summoned again." He rubbed the back of his neck. "I don't know much more about it than that."

I looked at him. "We're going to have to talk to O'Malley some more," I said, "but I'd like to wait to see if he finds anything from the summoner archives."

"I agree," my partner said.

There was a moment of silence before Jackson said what everyone had to be thinking and I hadn't wanted to. "I think we have to work on the theory that while the man who hurt Nykk is dead, maybe he was possessed by a demon who has been summoned again."

And there it was. I took a slow breath through my nose and saw everyone watching me closely, or maybe I just felt like they were. "I wouldn't swear to it without some kind of proof other than my face, but it does seem very likely." Even if I didn't like the thought, I had to concede the point. The room felt like it had grown a little smaller and a little hotter. I wanted to move on, though I knew it would be wrong to try to do so entirely. I was a cop, and just because I was uncomfortable was no reason not to be thorough with my job. "So, we have this information and it's good to know, but without more from O'Malley, is there actually something we can do with it?" I asked, working on being rational.

"Unfortunately, none that I can think of. They've started setting up a system for summoners, and animators, to be licensed, but that's not in place yet, and even if it was, that doesn't mean there couldn't be people practicing without a license." Vance paused before continuing. "Still, it's something useful to have and hopefully Donovan will come up with something. I'll keep on top of him, since he knows me anyways, and see what he finds. In the meantime, we still have other angles to work." He looked at Jackson and Kai.

"Did you guys turn anything up?"

"Yes and no," Jackson replied. He moved around a desk to reach a computer, tapping a few keys and pulling up some information. "The car reported stolen is registered to a Janet Meyers. We have a driver's license, so we have a photo, but the woman is apparently a ghost. There's just no trace of her. All the information given to the DMV turns up nothing. We have her photo circulating all the stations in the area, but frankly, I'm not hopeful."

"It's probably not even her real name," I muttered, stifling a sigh. "Still, maybe something will pop."

I decided I needed a cup of coffee, because I just wasn't buzzing enough. Leaving the others to return to their efforts, I went into the breakroom. I bopped the temperamental coffeemaker once for good measure, or maybe just because I had nothing else to hit, and then poured myself a cup of barely warm, barely tolerable dark substance that had been made that morning. I felt my face twist up around the taste of it but kept drinking anyways.

After a couple of minutes, the door behind me opened and closed, and Jackson appeared. I met his eyes over the rim of my cup, but just for a moment. I knew he was in here because he wanted to talk, but I didn't think I did. Then again, I never did, so that was a safe bet.

He didn't say anything, though, and I found that to be far more unsettling. He didn't pour himself a cup either, but I found that to be smart. Leaning back against the counter, he folded his arms and just looked.

"What?" I finally asked, frowning.

"Just wondering if you might finally like to talk," he said. "I know it's been more than fifteen years, but not through fault of either of us. We used to be really good friends."

How could a friendship survive silence for so long, and then all I'd been through during that time? I didn't know if it could, and I didn't see how he thought it could either... so why was he here talking to me like it was possible? And yet, the longer he stood there, the more I remembered the boy he used to be. He really didn't look that different, just a little taller and a little wider and with a five o'clock shadow. Oh, and the pyrokinesis...but that didn't matter right then. What mattered was how he looked at me, and the rush of memories back to the fourteen-year-old girl, sitting on the hill outside of town, looking at the lights of our little city. I saw him leaning into me and felt my heart jump as he kissed me. Young love, so long ago and all but buried until he walked back into my life.

Not that I felt a resurgence of that emotion. Not at all. But I did remember how close we'd been. He had been my best friend. I'd told him everything.

"This bothers the ever-living hell out of me, Jack," I said quietly, reverting to the name I'd called him when we were younger as I put away the cup of terrible black stuff, only charitably referred to as coffee. "I've been telling myself and everyone else that I'm okay, that this couldn't be the same guy because the guy who did this to me is dead, but what if what this summoner says is true? There was a demon inside Master and that demon might still be alive." I realized a half-dozen too many words too late what I'd said, what I'd called him, but it was too late to take it back. I just hoped he wouldn't bring it up.

He didn't, at least not in words. He looked at me for a long silent moment, but then looked away. "I have no idea how hard a thought that has to be for you," he said. "I can't even begin to imagine. But try to think of it like this, it doesn't really change anything in this case. We don't know how to track a demon, so it's just a piece of information, and the man, the hands, that actually hurt you *is* dead."

It didn't help any, but I didn't know how to explain. He was right. He didn't know what it was like, and he couldn't possibly. And yet, he was trying to be nice to me, to be comforting, to get me to open up. It was Jackson. I didn't want to push him away. If no one else, I didn't want to push *him* away.

"I just don't understand any of it," I changed my tact a little. "Demon or not, this thing had to be summoned by humans. People called on it and are letting it use them to do these terrible things. Cops are supposed to have some kind of insight, and I suppose I should have more than most, but I don't. I don't understand why this person is hurting these innocent girls, and I don't understand why—" I almost called him Master again. "—the man who hurt me did this to me."

"Psychologists will say a lot of things," Jackson said. "Kai will too, with her behavioral science background, but I don't know if it's true or just bullshit. Maybe there's just evil in the world, and that's as much explanation as there is."

It was a thought I'd naturally had before. I sighed. "I suppose you're right," I said, "but that doesn't make it any easier being on the hurt side of it."

He smiled kindly. He'd always had a really kind way about him. He'd always been a good man, even when he was still a boy. "I don't suppose it does."

Feebly, I tried to return the smile. My face wasn't really meant for smiling anymore, though. Then a whim possessed me. "Do you want to come over to my house for dinner tonight? You know, catch up?" I don't know what came over me, but once the words were out of my mouth, there was no taking them back. Maybe it wouldn't be such a bad thing, though. Maybe I could use...a friend. Maybe...my therapist was right.

"I'd like that," he said.

I thought I might, too.

CHAPTER SEVENTEEN

The workday concluded without any great leads, any answers, or anything that would do anything useful for us. It was disheartening, but sometimes that happened in this job. For some reason, it hit me harder that time. That was bullshit. It wasn't 'for some reason.' I knew precisely why it bothered me more in this case than in any other, but I couldn't do anything about it.

Jackson followed me home, upon my invitation. He wasn't stalking me or anything. He could leave after dinner without me having to drive him back to the station for his car that way, and that suited us both.

I left him to get comfortable in my living room while I went next door and picked up my sister. I was first greeted by a dog without a face, as Ana would put it, who turned out to be a Boston Terrier that could practically propel itself off its hind feet to reach my face and slurp all over it. I didn't entirely mind, though, because it was kind of so ugly it was cute.

All the way along the short walk back to our house, I got pelted with requests for a dog, until she saw Jackson.

"Who's this?" she asked with wide-eyed, innocent pleasure. We didn't have guests too often, almost ever aside from Mrs. Bauer. This was a novelty.

"You may not remember," he said with a charming smile, "but your sister and I knew each other back when we were kids. I knew you too, though my family moved away when you were still pretty little."

She tilted her head, like she was working on remembering. And it didn't work because she shook her head. "Sorry."

Jackson chuckled. "It's all right," he said. "I'm not surprised. Like I said, it was a long time ago."

I watched how easily he talked with my sister and remembered the warm kid he'd been. Not everyone handled Ana well, and less in ways I approved of. Her physical appearance made it obvious that she wasn't quite like everyone else, and it made it obvious what the major difference was, and people reacted to her differently. Usually not in a good way, as I'd learned myself. Most people treated her like a little kid, when she wasn't psychologically at that level. I hated that. But Jackson talked to her like a person, like she was my sister who just happened to have Down Syndrome.

I kind of loved him right there. Not really in any romantic sense, but just as another human being. In my line of work, I didn't find a whole lot of those.

Tossing a frozen pizza in the oven, I steered everyone into the living room. Ana and Jackson kept talking. I kind of hung around the edges, just watching and listening and finding myself wondering if this was what a "normal" life would be like. If it was, I thought it wouldn't be such a bad gig. I just couldn't see how it could ever truly be *my* life.

"Are you Nykk's boyfriend?"

Ana's sudden question and change in direction brought me up short and judging from Jackson's sudden throat-clearing, it seemed to do the same to him. He looked at me briefly before chuckling, shaking his head. "No, we're just friends and colleagues," he said a bit more suavely than I would have managed.

My sister looked a little crestfallen. "Oh, okay. I just

thought you're nice. And she's never brought a boy home for dinner before."

I felt the skin around my facial scars tightening as blood rushed to my cheeks. I should have seen it coming, but I hadn't. Any reply I had to make was preempted by the ringing of the stove, which I rushed with undue haste to get to. Conversation in the living room seemed to lag for a few moments, but then picked up again as it had done previously and I let out a sigh of relief.

Ana wasn't wrong. I didn't bring "boys" home for dinner, but I didn't bring anyone home for dinner. Vance had stopped by once to drop something off, but Sadie had been with him, and the vampire's presence—while bringing up a lot of other questions from my curious sister—had stymied any thoughts of dating.

Cutting up the pizza, I just crossed my fingers this would be the last of it and called them to the table. The square of wood usually only housed two, but three wasn't too bad a fit. Silence descended for a while as we started eating.

"So how come you're not Nykk's boyfriend?" Ana asked in between bites.

I nearly choked.

Jackson patted my back as I coughed as quietly as I could into a paper towel, trying to keep my dinner from ending up in my sinus cavity. While I was preoccupied, he saved me again. "There's no particular reason. We just aren't dating, but we are friends. Not every man and woman who're friends have to be boyfriend and girlfriend, too."

"Oh, I know that," she said with a nod. "There's a boy at work I'm friends with, but we aren't dating. I wouldn't want to date him."

"Why not?" he asked.

She frowned a little and then shrugged. "I just wouldn't. 'Cause we're friends."

He smiled. "That's what it's like for your sister and I."

Ana thought about this for a moment and then nodded, apparently accepting the rationale and moving on. She started asking more questions about his being a federal cop instead of a "regular" one like me. I went back to eating normally, relieved I'd dodged the bullet twice. I just wasn't good with questions like that. I didn't know what to say: sorry, sis, I don't imagine I'll ever have a man over, because who'd want to look at this face every day across a pillow?

We finished dinner, and they both helped me with the dishes. As it had been late to begin with, Ana went to her room to watch some television on her own and then go to bed. Jackson and I took up residence on the couch and had a chance to talk to one another, as I'd been predominantly silent through the evening so far.

Apparently, he'd noticed. "Everything all right?" he asked. I nodded. "Your sister is really sweet."

"Yeah, she is." I smiled a little. "Sometimes I don't know what to do with her, though. I hope her questions, about being my boyfriend and all, didn't bother you."

With one ankle resting across his knee, he looked easy and relaxed. I envied that ability. "Not at all," he said warmly, shaking his head. "I'm one of five and have a bunch of nieces and nephews. You get used to stuff like that."

I remembered his family, although the youngest had been just a toddler when I was kidnapped. I couldn't remember if it had been a boy or a girl. "Is your family still in California?"

He nodded. "Most of them. My younger sister, Joy, and her family ended up in Texas. Her husband is in the Air Force, and they got moved there a few years ago. Poor thing, she's got not one but two sets of twins, six and three."

My eyes widened. "That's got to be hell."

Jackson laughed. "It certainly can be, but they're

good kids." He paused. "Of the five of us, I'm the only one without kids who's really old enough to have them. Camille is the youngest, and she's only eighteen. While I get that technically that's old enough, she's too scared of my mother to get knocked up without being married." He smirked.

I tried to picture his family, from what I remembered, but I hadn't met them that often. My thoughts drifted, like a mental connect-the-dots. "I don't even know if my brother has kids. I doubt it. He doesn't seem like the type, but I really can't be sure."

"When was the last time you talked to him?"

"I think we talked a few months after Mom died," I replied, thinking back. "That was shortly after I graduated college, so about seven or eight years ago. I've sent him letters sometimes, but he never writes back."

Jackson frowned. "What happened?"

Embarrassed, I looked down at my hands. I didn't know what it was about the night, but I was suffering a deplorable excess of honesty. "My getting taken kind of broke my family. My dad had a heart attack and died while I was being kept. Mom wasn't ever the same. Ana didn't get all the help she needed. Peter kind of just got left out. Mom was happy to have me back, but she couldn't handle it. I went to live with an aunt. Peter said once that I came back, but Mom never did."

"That's not your fault, Nykk."

"I know." I shrugged, because it wasn't that simple. I didn't ask to be abducted, of course, but it was all because of me.

He reached out and put his hand on mine, not in any sort of romantic way, just compassionately, as he said, "I'm sorry, Nykk." But his pyrokinesis must have been up and his hand was really hot. I yelped a little and drew it back fast. Memories of being burned flooded my mind, and I froze on the couch, staring at him for a painfully long moment.

Jackson grimaced and repeated the earlier sentiment for new reasons. "Oh, hell, Nykk, I'm really sorry. Sometimes I get a little warmer than I mean to."

"It's okay." But I sounded more breathless than I wanted to. Unwanted memories still rushed around in the front of my brain.

He must have read something in my expression. "Maybe I should go," he said, his smile weaker than before, rueful. Part of me wanted to tell him to stay, that I did enjoy his company, but the part controlling my mouth wasn't it. I watched as he got up, and I managed to follow him and offer a polite half-smile as he left, but my brain had kicked into overdrive.

Shutting the door behind him, I leaned against it, pressing my hot forehead to the cold glass as I listened to his car start and drive away. I wished I could have told him not to go, but all I could do was try to stop the memories from pulling me under.

Chapter Eighteen

I didn't sleep well that night.

At least four different nightmares woke me up in a cold sweat, and I repeated my calming ritual for every one, but it took longer each time to get back to sleep. By the time my alarm went off, I'd been staring at the clock for nearly twenty minutes.

Getting Ana up and fed and off to work passed in a haze. I managed to get some food shopping done without accidentally ramming my cart into anyone else's and by the time I was at check-out, I started feeling like a human being again. Mostly. I got stuff home and unpacked, put a load of dishes in the washer, and then went to work.

Everyone was already there when I arrived. I had a little trouble meeting Jackson's eye, but I was grateful he didn't press the issue. I knew I'd have to talk to him and tell him it wasn't his fault, but I wasn't quite ready for it. I wanted to focus on work. Not that work wasn't reminding me of the past enough, but at least I could put myself into their lives and crawl out of my own.

"Do we have anything?" I asked, although I wasn't hopeful.

"There's been nothing about the car or its driver," Vance said, waving a folder without much in it. "We did just get a call from Wright, and he'd like us to come down because he's got something for us."

I snorted. "That's just the way to start off a day," I

muttered. "A trip to the morgue."

He chuckled, although it was a somewhat mirthless sound. The lack of useful leads and information—all the while having four tormented, cold faces staring at us—was taking its toll on everyone. "I know how to show a girl a good time," he joked and then nodded at the door. "Come on, best not keep the good doctor waiting. Lang, Kai, are you coming?"

Jackson looked at Vance, then me, then Vance again. "You guys can let us know what you hear. We'll keep working things from this side."

Shrugging, Vance walked out the door, and I followed.

I realized I wasn't feeling as awkward as I had thought I would. Exhausted as all hell, but not awkward or tense. I think he thought I was, so I'd have to let him know it wasn't the case when I got back. He didn't need to be worried about that any longer than necessary.

Once we were in the car and on our way, Vance looked at me. "Everything okay?"

I blinked, wondering what he knew. "Yeah, why?"

"You look like hell, for one," he replied, eyes on the road. "And Lang has been looking at you kind of funny. Just want to make sure things are all right."

"Things are fine," I said, smiling weakly and looking out the window. Although we'd become friends, I still was never sure where the appropriate line was. In this case, I elected to leave it at that. If he wanted to ask anything else, he made the same choice and nothing more was said on the matter.

We got to the morgue and found Cor in the lab. "Wright is busy right now, but he asked me to tell you what's going on." He waved us in closer. "We found something on the tape used to close the plastic on the Davidson girl." I liked how he got right to the point. He tapped out something on a keyboard and read the results off the monitor in front of him. "There were traces of motor oil and flower pollen."

Vance and I exchanged a look. That was new. "Neither of those things have shown up before, have they?"

Cor shook his head. "No. It sounds like the killer is starting to get sloppy." He read for another moment. "We identified the pollen as *symphyotrichum novae-angliae*, also known as the New England Aster. It happens to be a fall blooming flower, so wherever this girl was wrapped up, these asters will be nearby."

I wasn't sure how much this knowledge would help us, but it was better than nothing. If the killer was getting sloppy, and that sounded accurate according to the number of clues starting to add up, then that was going to help us.

With that information in our back pocket, I had to ask something else. "Have you guys figured out any cause for the damage to girls' brains?"

The M.E. straightened up and crossed his arms over his chest, shaking his head. "I'm afraid not."

"We're looking into a theory that there's a demon at work here," I said, although the word tasted bad in my mouth and dredged up those thoughts I didn't like. "Could the damage have been caused by magical means?"

"Of course it's possible," he replied without hesitation. "The use of magic as an option means almost anything is. For example, genetically speaking, we've been able to trace biological sources for everything about shifters, but still no clue about what animates vampires. Other than magic, which we can't see under our microscopes."

Vance spoke up, "There isn't any way to...test for it?" We were both out of our league when it came to the details of the inner workings of biology and science.

Cor shook his head again. "Not through any mean of ours," he said. "Determining the cause as magic comes in one of two ways. Either it's a process of elimination, where nothing else makes sense, or we have to use magic to figure it out."

There was another look exchanged. This was more Vance's field than mine, and I could have sworn I saw the wheels turning inside his head. Something clicked after a moment, and he looked back at the young doctor. "Are any of the bodies undamaged enough to be animated?"

"Davidson," he said, again replying without hesitation. "She was the least damaged over all, having spent the least amount of time in captivity."

Something about the easy way he said that sent a shiver down my spine, but I knew I shouldn't blame him. Disassociating from the crime was likely the only way to deal with it, but I had to wonder if the doctors in the hospital sounded like that when they talked about me, or if the M.E. looking at my corpse—had I died—would've been that way.

I shook that thought off and turned to the topic at hand. The details of animation were beyond me, but I knew what I had to. "We'll have to get the permission of her mother," I said with a faint grimace. "We have to do it, but I don't look forward to that conversation." In fact, I was hoping I wouldn't have to. Maybe Jackson could go with Vance. The two of them were obviously better at such things than I was. I'd see if I could talk them into it when the time came.

With nothing more to say, we thanked Cor and left the morgue.

❨❍❩

When we got back into the parking lot, we saw a woman leaning against the driver's side of our car. She had that casual air of belonging wherever she happened to be standing and we recognized her right away.

"Andrea Sullivan, what the hell are you doing here?" Vance asked, although it wasn't with any particular malice.

"I've told you before, Detective, to call me Andy," she replied, still leaning against our car with her hands over her chest.

Andrea "Andy" Sullivan was the lead reporter for the Adelheid Chronicle. With a dark complexion, ever-present smirk, and an eye for details like a bird of prey, she was very good at her job. She also happened to sprout feathers every full moon, but I didn't think too much about that one way or the other. She was a reporter, and therefore a pain in the ass by nature.

Matching her posture without the leaning, Vance crossed his thick arms over his chest. "You didn't answer my question, *Andy*," he said wryly. "What the hell are you doing here?"

Her dark brows arched. "Are you serious? You are the detectives working on the biggest case in town. You're working with the FBI, for heaven's sake. Where else would I be but trying to get information out of you?"

"You know we can't tell you anything," I said flatly. I didn't have anything against her personally, and reporters had their place, but I wasn't in the mood for a journalistic tango. I rarely was, really.

"Are you sure?" Those hawk eyes zeroed in on me, and I almost took a step back out of instinct, but I stopped myself. "I hear you've got yourself four bodies sitting cold in that morgue over there with weird-ass scars that look an awful lot like yours, Detective Marlowe."

I knew that after the senator's press conference, the scarring wasn't a secret, but he hadn't shown pictures. How did she know what the scars looked like, and that it looked like me? Her knowledge wasn't impossible to get, I knew, but her saying it so casually made the hackles go up a little.

"We don't have anything to say, Ms. Sullivan," I said tightly.

"Now that's a 'no comment' at its finest," Vance came in, probably sensing the rigidity in my tone and posture and wanting to keep it from getting any worse.

Andy pursed her lips slightly. "You can't tell me anything?" she pressed. "This is a big story, and everyone is clamoring for more information. The daughter of a prominent senator is the victim of a serial killer and one who may well have ties to a detective working the case. It's like a story from a mystery novel."

All of her words put together were enough to make my spine tighten further, like a coil slowly being wound. I wanted to shout that this wasn't the same guy and there wasn't any connection. I wanted to scream that the only thing tying me to those dead girls was a really fucked-up twist of fate. I wanted to just scream, but I didn't let myself. It was a struggle, but I held it off.

"No comment," I managed instead.

"Is it true that they're all blonde?"

"No comment." This time from Vance.

"Just one quote," she pressed, flashing a smile. "I'll give you the cover story."

Vance put his hands on either side of her shoulders and slid her away from the driver's side door with a smile. "No comment," he repeated and then got in.

She turned her attention to me, but apparently there was a look on my face that she could read and turned away from. If nothing else, Andy Sullivan was smart and had a strong survival instinct. I knew she'd spent time in jail for contempt of court after refusing to reveal sources because of their paranormal nature, prior to Cameron's Law. With a resigned nod, she stepped away. I got in the car, and we went back to the office.

CHAPTER NINETEEN

Neither of us said anything on the drive back. I needed to sort my brain back out before I could work again, and Vance either sensed that or just didn't have anything to say. Either way, I wasn't complaining.

Once we got back to the office, I followed him to the station door. "Do you think you can handle getting permission from Crystal Davidson's mother for the animation?" I asked, not looking at him as I did.

He held the door for me. An outdated gesture, but I appreciated it all the same. I didn't usually inspire chivalrous instincts in men. "Sure," he said, not asking why I wanted him to do it. He could probably guess. Over the course of our partnership, it was no secret I was not the "heart" of the pair. Gender stereotypes did not live here.

In the squad room, he went straight to the phone, and I updated our federal friends about the news from the M.E.'s office, as well as the visit from our local reporter. Not that it would matter much to them, they knew the party line just as well as we did, but I wanted to give them the heads-up all the same.

From there, it was rather boring. Anyone who watches all of those crime shows on television probably thinks that things happen fast and there are always shoot-outs, car chases, and someone shouting whatever urban "eureka" equivalent there was for that show's demographic. Sadly, that's not the case in real life. It can be remarkably boring, filled with a lot of time deep in paper and on the phone.

"We got her permission," Vance said after a little while, hanging up his handset. I could see a worn expression at the corners of his eyes and imagined it hadn't been an easy phone call. How many mothers would rejoice at the idea of the artificial animation of their dead daughter? I just hoped it would give us the information we needed and wouldn't all be for nothing.

Now all we had to do was wait for dark, because no animator worked in the daylight.

At one point, I went to get a cup of coffee in the breakroom and found myself suddenly face to face and alone with Jackson. I tried not to look surprised, but I probably failed miserably.

"I wanted to apologize for last night," he said.

"I already told you it was okay," I replied. What else was I supposed to say? I was just having a moment of bat-shit crazy and not to worry about it? Actually, that probably would have worked, but I didn't actually want to say it. "You just caught me off guard, and I'm not a fan of things getting too hot."

He nodded slowly. He wanted to ask. I could see it all over his face. For several moments, I warred with myself about whether I wanted to tell him. Apparently, I did. I glanced around to make sure we were still alone, but I lowered my voice anyway. "I got burned a lot, back then." I didn't feel like being police-specific. He obviously got what I meant because the questions vanished from his eyes.

"Well, now I'm *really* sorry," he said with a weak smile.

"Really, don't worry about it. It's not like you had any idea or did it on purpose, right?"

"Right."

"Then don't worry about it." I forced a small smile to try to make him feel better, and also find a way to stop this conversation.

He nodded slowly, a little doubtfully, but didn't seem like he was going to pursue it any further. "All right," he said. "Well, if I promise to not light anything on fire, maybe we can do dinner again sometime."

I managed another small smile. "Sure, we can do that."

After he nodded again and left the room, I let out a sigh of relief, and then wondered why I had. Didn't his leaving just mean I could go back to worrying about who was capturing, torturing, and killing teenage girls? Dealing with a small misunderstanding and dinner with an old friend really should have been preferred.

☾○☽

Once it was dark, we were able to go the Stanton Agency... again. This time, we were looking for Sarah Beaumont. She was the agency's animator and a quick phone call assured that she would be there when we arrived, saving us from having to scour local graveyards until we found her.

Madison led us into her office. Sarah sat behind her desk, looking through a file with her brows knit. She was an average-looking woman, taller than me, with short brown hair kept back from her face. You'd never guess by looking at her that she raised the dead for a living, but I supposed, for her, that was a good thing.

The office was nondescript with the most prominent feature being a second person in the room. He was sitting on the couch, impatiently flipping through a magazine. We'd met him before, back when he first started at the agency. His name was D. He wouldn't tell anyone but Sadie his full name, and that was a little obnoxious, but it wasn't really my business, was it? He was a vampire and Sarah's bodyguard.

Some of the local bigots objected to zombies and the

people who made them.

He looked up at us when we walked in. His face was mostly impassive, though maybe a little annoyed. Perhaps we were holding them up. But then again, he always kind of had that look in his eyes. It was predatory.

I ignored him and looked at Sarah, who was looking up now. "Sadie said you had to ask me something?" she asked politely.

"We need you to raise a body," I said. "It's for a police matter."

She nodded easily, because it wasn't uncommon for the cops to get the help of animators. There were others in town we worked with, though, when Sarah wasn't available, but she was one of the best so we usually went to her first. Smiling a little, she waved at the empty chairs in front of her desk. We sat down, although I got a twitch putting my back to D, even though I didn't *really* think he'd do anything. "Tell me more about the case."

We did so, but with as little information as we could. She would possibly be privy to more than we wanted if the animating worked, but that didn't mean we wanted to dump our entire playbook on the table ahead of time. She listened patiently and didn't interrupt.

"I wish I could help, Detective," she began doubtfully once we had finished, "but that is a lot of brain damage to work through. For the information you want, we need the brain as intact as we can get it. I'm not sure I can do it, or if anyone could."

"You should give yourself more credit," a deep voice with a faint southern accent came from the previously silent vampire behind us.

She smiled. "I appreciate the vote of confidence, D, but I'm trying to be realistic."

Vance leaned forward, forearms across the edge of the

desk. I thought I heard D shift on the couch behind us, but he said nothing and didn't leave his seat. "Sarah," Vance began, "do you think you could at least try? I get that it's not likely, but we're running on empty here and need something. This is the fourth victim, and we have no sign of stopping this killer."

The animator still looked doubtful, but she didn't say no.

"These are just kids," Vance went on. He saw his advantage and pressed it. "Can it hurt to try? Isn't the worst that can happen is nothing happens?"

"I suppose so," Sarah granted with a sigh. "I have a little time before my first appointment. I will try, but understand I make no promises at all. It's unlikely to achieve the results you want."

Vance smiled slightly. "That's all we ask."

I sighed with relief, but why then did I suddenly feel this knot in my gut?

Fourth Interlude

She's fidgeting now, apparently still having trouble keeping still. "Time lost all meaning. After I was back, they told me it had been about eleven months from the time I was taken till the time I was rescued. I know they aren't lying, but it didn't seem like that. You know? I thought it had been eleven years, or maybe just eleven hours. The basement was dark, and I couldn't really see the sun or the moon. I never knew when it was day or night, just when it hurt and when it didn't."

"Tell me about when you were rescued."

"I'm told that a woman passing by the house heard me scream. Master had told me to be quiet, but one time, I couldn't help myself." She covers her face with her hands and sighs deeply. "I was so afraid he'd be angry. I couldn't bear the idea he'd be upset with me." Pulling her hands away, she meets your eyes, briefly. "He was all I had. You understand, right? I couldn't make him angry, because he was all."

You nod slowly. "I understand." Whether you do or not really makes no difference, because she needs unconditional support now. Though you do understand a little. As best you can without having lived it.

"Thank you," she says softly. "Anyways, a woman heard me scream. People didn't often walk so close to that house, but she had and she called the cops. I don't know all the details." She turns her head, and a distance enters her expression, drawing her more deeply into herself. "I just know I heard the commotion upstairs. They were shouting that they were the

police. I was terrified. Master shouted. I don't know what he said, but soon, there were three gunshots and a heavy thud.

"They came down the stairs. I wanted to crawl under my table, but I couldn't. There were people and hands and eyes and looks and words everywhere. I had a hard time understanding what was going on. I was untied and pulled off the table, carried upstairs. I remember the sun was so bright it burned my eyes. I hadn't seen the sun for almost a year. It hurt so much.

"I just remember it was all glaring light and loud noises and pain."

CHAPTER TWENTY

We all took a field trip down to the morgue. The place was creepy in the daylight and worse at night, even to a police officer. Everyone had been here at one time or another, so the four of us made our way without any trouble. D maintained his presence as a silent but unmistakable shadow in our wake.

Having gotten our call, Crystal Davidson was laid out on a table in a room alone, and there were no employees of the morgue in there. I knew the place wasn't closed for business, because nothing closed at night in Adelheid, but they were keeping a discreet distance and giving us room to work.

The knot in the center of my body had wound tighter as we got there. I felt a little bit of adrenaline surging through my system, making me want to run away and not hear what this girl might say, but I kept my place. I wanted her to talk and give us a clue, but I didn't want to hear what she said.

Sarah looked distinctly uncomfortable. She preferred graveyards to work in over the sterility of a morgue. It was weird, but I kept that to myself.

Davidson had been pretty in life, but now the tendrils of scars crept up her face in raw red lines. They were barely scars at this point, more like freshly healed wounds, but I knew what they would have become if she had been given the chance to live. Would she have been able to live with them, or would she have hated herself forever?

Taking an audible deep breath, Sarah came up to the

side of the table. Her eyes fixed steadily on the waxy face, and she put her hands at either side of the head but without touching. With another breath, Sarah's body stilled, and a look of concentration filled her features as she worked. I wasn't supernatural so I couldn't feel what was going on, but I saw Vance rub his arms through his sleeves like he was calming goosebumps, and D took a breath behind us. Since vampires don't breathe, I took it for a sign that Sarah's magic was at work.

And yet, nothing happened.

I watched closely as Sarah's hands began to tremble with her effort, fingers going pale and brows knitting. Her teeth sunk into her lower lip while there were more breaths behind me, and Vance clutched his hands around either forearm, frowning. It was strange, knowing something was happening but having almost no way to judge it for myself. Even so, I could tell by what I saw and heard, and it made the knot grow tighter, drawing all the muscles of my body inward.

"I don't know..." Sarah began, her voice breathless and tight, but then the air seemed to vibrate for an instant. Something snapped all around us. Even I felt it.

Gasping, Sarah clutched her own head and fell back several steps. D rushed with vampire speed to grab her before she knocked into the tables and shelves behind her. Vance and I would have checked on her, but the girl on the table let out an inhuman shriek and sat bolt upright.

Her limbs thrashed like she was fighting someone. The actual movements were feeble, but you could tell she was fighting with all the strength she thought she had against someone only she could see. She screamed and screamed in ways I didn't know, even with my history, a person could. It froze us all in place as she screamed until her head snapped back with violent suddenness, like...

Like she had just been thrown off a building with a

noose around her neck.

"Crystal Davidson?" Vance was the first of us to overcome the shock.

"Yes," she gasped, voice grating through a broken larynx. "Are you here to save me?"

Something in my soul cracked.

"We're going to help you," Vance said sincerely. "Can you tell us where you are?" He effortlessly moved with the scenario and spoke to her like she was still captive, because in her mind, she always would be.

I knew it.

"No... No..." She started breathing, it rasped from her chest. Her head still hung back, like it would never be straight again. "There are others. Are you still there?! Katerina, talk to me! Mary Ellen, don't be afraid. Oh God." She sobbed, sounds choked by the unnatural angle of her neck.

My eyes snapped around and instantly met Vance's gaze. Mary Ellen? Our thoughts were the same. None of the girls we'd found had been named Mary Ellen. It seemed obvious.

There was another girl.

We would have rushed out that instant, but our horrific conversation was not over.

"Don't cry, don't cry. The flowers, can you smell the flowers? I can smell the flowers. Don't cry, don't cry. What are you doing to me? Why are you doing this? No, please, not again. It hurts, it hurts. Why are you doing this? I will be quiet, I promise, I promise, just please stop hurting me. Where are you taking her?! No! Come back, please, stop, don't take her! Don't take her! Don't..."

Her words started mixing with incoherent sounds, unintelligible words, until they dissolved all together into a new barrage of ragged screams. Each one drove down into me and made my scars, from hip to hairline, pulse and burn.

"Sarah," Vance called, finally looking over his shoulder.

I looked too and saw the animator breathing heavily, leaning against a table with D hovering protectively. She heard Vance call her and stepped forward, putting her hand before Davidson's screaming face. "Sleep," she commanded, and the body fell back, inert, against the table.

☾○☽

After that, we all needed some air.

Despite the November chill, we sat outside on the curb at the back of the building. People rarely drove down this road. We only had a minute, I knew, because we had to get back to the station and find out if this Mary Ellen was a missing girl, or maybe the kidnapper or an accomplice. But for the moment, we had to breathe.

Vance was looking sidelong at Sarah. "Are you okay?" I finally realized what he had hooked into, which was that Sarah looked very pale.

"Yeah," she said quietly. "I... Something happened with my power. I didn't think I was going to be able to, but suddenly..." She shook her head.

"She leveled up," D said with a half-smirk.

We both looked at him curiously. "She what?"

His gaze remained on Sarah. I would have thought it might be romantic, but I knew it wasn't. Vance could be a good source of information about that sort of thing, really, and I knew D was just a good bodyguard. "She's a necromancer."

Vance's eyes showed clear understanding, but I was left in the dust. I was twitching to get back to the office, but I had to ask, "What's the difference?"

"Power," Sarah answered me distantly. "Necromancers are far more powerful. I could control a vampire now, if I wanted."

D shuddered, but with a touch of the theatric.

"Hell of a night," I said with a shudder of my own. "I don't know if congratulations are in order, so...whatever I should say in this situation then let's say I said it." They all managed a half-laugh for that one. I turned to Vance. "We gotta get back now."

I had to know if there was another girl out there.

CHAPTER TWENTY-ONE

I felt like a ping pong ball between the office and other points in town, which was usually how it went but it seemed like everything was more pronounced now. Everything I felt and thought was sharper and dug down deeper. My scars still ached when we walked into the squad room, and it took all I had to not wince in pain when they throbbed as we reported the happenings at the morgue.

"From how you describe the way she spoke," Kai began thoughtfully, "it does sound like this Mary Ellen is another victim, rather than a perpetrator." She brushed aqua hair back off her shoulders.

"Is there another body we haven't found, then?" Jackson said. It was obvious in his expression that he didn't like the idea.

Whether my idea was better or worse was up for debate. "Or she's still alive."

The stack of missing girls that had been pulled earlier wasn't huge, but dividing it between four people made it go much quicker. The one "hit" was in my pile, however, and I caught everyone's attention. "Mary Ellen James," I read out loud. "She's fifteen, within our height range and body type, blonde. She was reported missing in July by her parents." I looked up and suddenly felt like there was a fire in my belly.

She might still be alive.

To know you're racing against a clock to stop a killer from grabbing someone else is one thing. To know the killer is out there with another victim in hand is something else, putting to mind the idea of that victim standing on the edge of a precipice. You have to move quickly to make sure she's not pushed off.

"That's two months after the Davidson girl. It seems like all of the girls were kept at least six months, and that was Davidson," Jackson did the math and said out loud what I was thinking.

"But our killer is cleaning house now, it seems," Kai pointed out.

"Let's try to be optimistic," Vance said. "She could still be alive, and that means we have a chance of saving her." He looked around and met each of our eyes. "Let's go talk to her parents."

I nodded. Although I'd been averse to talking with families in the previous cases, this time I wanted to go. Maybe it was the idea of being able to tell them that their child might be alive, rather than just telling them their child was dead. Then again, how did you tell parents that their child might be alive, being tortured until some unknown time when she would be hanged?

Whatever it was, I volunteered to go. Mary Ellen James lived just outside of Adelheid. We called ahead and her parents were home, so we were received upon arrival.

"Do you have any news?" her distraught mother asked quickly. We weren't even through the door yet.

"We aren't sure," Vance asked tactfully. "We believe we might have a lead, but please understand we don't want to get your hopes up by saying too much. We wanted to talk to you and refresh ourselves on the facts of the case."

It was all over the mother's face that she wanted to ask questions, but she restrained herself. The father didn't say much, just looked tired. "What do you want to know?" the mother asked.

They agreed to let us see Mary Ellen's bedroom while we talked. I let him take care of the talking part. I listened while I looked around. I tried not to disturb anything, just observe and seek out any clues.

"Mary was grounded," the mother was explaining as she stood in the doorway with the father, like they couldn't bear to go in the room. "I can't even remember what it was for." She laughed weakly. "I think she broke curfew. She was just grounded for a few days, but could be headstrong. Thought she was in love. She snuck out one afternoon. We figured it was...it was to see her boyfriend."

"Did the cops talk to him?" Vance asked. I was sure we'd check for ourselves, too.

The bedroom looked like the room of any average fifteen-year-old. The furniture was white, not expensive but not cheap, and the walls had been painted an insane shade of blue. There was a rug on the floor that didn't match the blankets, which didn't match the pillows and looked like a kid still trying to figure out what she was doing in life.

At her age, I was on the verge of the psychiatric ward.

"Yes, they spoke with him. He's not a bad boy," she was quick to clarify, "but they're kids and foolish. He's sixteen and has a car. He was ruled out as a suspect in any wrongdoing and said he never saw her that day. He had an alibi for the whole day." She sighed, but it came out with a shudder.

"I'm sorry to have to ask, but was there ever any indication that Mary Ellen was likely to run away?"

"She could be rebellious, certainly, but...but all of her things are still here. She kept her money in a glass box in the top drawer of her desk, and it's still there. Her laptop is still here. The only thing missing was her purse and whatever was in it, plus her phone. We tried calling, but of course we got no answer."

Two bookshelves lined one wall, both had to be over six

foot tall, painted two different colors. I looked over the books, and they snagged on something in my mind as I looked at several mystery and thriller authors. In fact, it predominated.

"Your daughter liked to read," I said.

There was a pause. I didn't turn around to look at them, but they probably thought I couldn't speak. They had done a pretty good job before of not staring at my scars and maybe thought no vocal cords went with it.

After clearing his throat, Dad spoke for the first time. "Yes, she did. She's an avid reader. There's a bookstore a little ways away that she spent a lot of time at."

Finally, I turned around. An idea burrowed into my consciousness. "Is it within walking distance?"

Both frowned, uncertain, but nodded.

☾O☽

"What are you thinking?" Vance asked as we walked to the car, having finished our conversation with the James family. There was an edge to his tone that suggested he had a clue already.

"It's a weird coincidence, don't you think, that all of the victims really enjoyed reading and liked to read the same kinds of books." We climbed into the car. I waited till he was behind the wheel and had the car started before going on, "Katerina was homeless and spent her time in a used bookstore. Crystal wrote fan mail to authors. Mary Ellen walked to the bookstore and has a six-foot-tall shelf full of the same type of stories."

He nodded as he pulled out onto the road. "One can't deny that, but my brain is still stretching with how that pertains to it all and how to use that to find them."

I didn't have any idea about that one either, but something was telling me it was an important connection.

Whether we understood it or not didn't affect its importance.

We drove to the bookstore, which wasn't a bad walk from the James' house and even better in summer than winter. It was a decent-sized store, but it wasn't one of the big chains. We didn't waste any time finding an employee and tracking down someone who had been working there last July.

"Do you have any recollection of seeing this girl here before?" Vance asked, showing him the picture of Mary Ellen we had on file. It was a long shot, with how many people this kid probably saw in a day, but we had to try.

He was tall, almost as tall as Vance, but only half his bulk. The nametag on his shirt read *Walter*. He took the picture. "Her," he said, eyes lighting after a moment. "I asked her out. She turned me down." He laughed like it didn't bother him, and it actually sounded like it was sincere. "Yeah, she used to come in here all the time. She'd browse the mystery section, ask about new authors, and sit in the café to read. Haven't seen her in a while, though, now that you mention it." The light bulb went off over his head as he seemed to make the connection. "What's wrong with her?" His eyes jumped between us, though lingered on me a moment longer each time they landed.

"We don't know," I answered honestly. "I don't suppose you recall seeing her last July, do you?"

"Jeez, I don't know." He frowned. Vance casually plucked the photo out of his stilled hands. "Yeah, I do. I remember she was chatting with some guy. Short, kinda bulky, kinda old, you know? Short dark hair. Didn't get a good look at the face, but I remembered thinking that if that was her type then I never had a shot." He paused. "I think she left with him, now that you mention it."

I tried to keep my reaction off my face. "Are you sure?"

He thought about it for a few moments and nodded. "Pretty sure." He looked down at his hand and frowned, realizing the picture was gone. He looked around like he was worried he'd dropped it before he saw it back in Vance's hand. "Saw them through the window, dark four-door, drove off toward Waterford."

Wheels clicked and pieces slid together. "Thank you, Walter, you've been very helpful." I managed to force a faint smile.

He smiled, but then it faded again. "I hope she's okay."

"I hope so too." Though I knew from experience that even if we found her alive, she'd never know his kind of okay again.

CHAPTER TWENTY-TWO

My mind buzzed as we left the store, but it was interrupted by the ringing of my cell phone.

"Marlowe."

"Detective," a voice I didn't immediately recognize began, "it's Donovan from the Stanton Agency." Now, I did. "I've been hard at work and think I may have something. I'm at the summoner archives in Hartford. Can you meet me here?"

That was about an hour drive, but if it led to information… I checked the time. It looked like Ana was staying with Mrs. Bauer tonight. I relayed the call to Vance. "Go and see what he has," he said. "I'll tell the others what we found out about James."

Getting back on the phone, I told him I'd be there.

Vance brought us back to the station so I could get my car, but I didn't even bother going inside. I got right back on the road and called Mrs. Bauer on the way. She was as understanding as always. I didn't know what I'd do if she wasn't my neighbor, with a schedule like mine.

The hour's drive was full of thoughts, but like a kaleidoscope, they were just fragments swirling around. All cases were the same, to a degree, with pieces of information floating, some fitting together and some not, some making sense and some not, but this was different. This was harder. The case itself was harder. The nature of it was more difficult than most, and anyone would agree, but they'd also be able to see in bright red that it was harder for me. It was easier to see all the pieces, but harder to make them fit together.

Before I knew it, I was in the state's capital. I drove to the address he'd given me and found myself in front of an old building. It had the age for the area, but not quite the stateliness of the more 'official' buildings near it. I parked in a narrow parking lot to one side, glad to not have to park on the street, and entered. There was no security system or guard, and I didn't even see any cameras, but I did feel a strange tingle on my skin as I walked in. I got the feeling that efforts beyond technology were at work here.

"Detective!" Donovan jogged up to me from the end of a long corridor. "Thanks for coming on such short notice. I just figured you should be here."

I nodded and fell into step with him as he led me through. "Thanks for calling me." We walked through the long stone hall and passed doors leading into rooms full of books so old I could see from a distance that they were nearly falling apart.

"Here's what I know," he began again as he led me into a big room that looked like any library or rare bookstore one might imagine. He gestured for me to have a seat at a table in the center, but he moved around and started grabbing books and scrolls—actual scrolls—and setting them on the table. "Remember what I told you before? That kind of mark only comes from a particular kind of demon."

"One who used to be human," I said, watching him moving around like a frantic spider or hyperactive child.

He nodded. "That's right, and that shit does not happen easy. We're talking major evil to summon a demon that can do that and then let them take you over. But like all demons, it's a deal. That deal just happens to, literally, be your soul." He finally sat down beside me, turning to look me in the eye. "The summoning itself won't cause any alerts, so to speak, but while the two are merged, bad things happen. Once the host body dies, the demon is expelled, but it takes the human's soul with it. The merging becomes permanent, and there are..." He paused, looking away like he was trying to find the right word. "There are ripples that can be felt by any summoner in the area."

I'd had no idea they could even do something like that. For a woman living in a paranormal city, I was pretty behind. "That's insane." Maybe not my best line, but it was the best I had.

Donovan didn't seem offended. In fact, he smiled darkly. "It is. It takes a very particular kind of human, a real degenerate, to be able to do this. Sometimes a demon will try, but the merging never happens." He paused. "Anyways, when the merging is successful and the new demon is created, the ripples go out. Summoners feel it. And even through all the centuries, we've kept good records." He gestured around us. "As you can see. Whenever any of them felt this kind of ripple, they wrote it down and investigated as best they could, but some of these records go back a long way and to times when doing that was very hard. Information can be spotty."

The man could talk, a lot. I kept up as best as I was able and, to his credit, he obviously worked to explain it so I could understand him but without sounding like he was talking to a three-year-old. And he was giving me important information.

"One thing that is important to know is that the same demon will keep doing it. We can't ever be sure where or how the demon started, but as long as it's summoned, it will keep looking for hosts to merge and take over, adding more souls and more energy and more power to itself as it goes. The only thing saving all of us from these types of demons is that it has to be summoned specifically. It can't just break into our realm and start grabbing people."

His choice of words triggered something in my brain. "Now it gets the body to do that." I said it before I could stop myself.

It took him a moment, but he got my meaning. His tan skin flushed slightly. "Sorry," he said but only let that sit for a moment before he moved on. "These are records from across the country and some European nations about summoners who've felt these ripples and what they were able to find out. A demon doesn't have to be tied to any specific physical location, so I wanted to give us as broad a range as we could."

I looked over the old books and scrolls. "That's good," I said, though I was imagining the asthma I was going to develop in the process.

Without any more explanation needed, apparently, we dove in. I wasn't entirely sure what I was looking for but hoped it would jump out at me when I saw it.

As it turned out, what jumped out at me for a while was that there were a lot of really sick fucks in the world. I already knew this, being a cop and all, but if I thought what I saw in my years on the job was bad, it was worse when combined with demonic atrocities. And that was demons being demons, of a certain type at least, but that these humans purposely let them inside and let them use them to do it...and then became part of the demon? It was kind of horrific. No, really, it was totally horrific.

Cases from all over the world rolled out before me with crimes of varying natures and frequency, but always heinous in some way or another. Information was, as Donovan had said, spottier on the earlier ones. I understood why, because the job of the summoners was a lot like a cop's. They came into the picture after it was done and had to backtrack, but the summoners couldn't ask the direct questions. They had to be discreet and covert to gather their information, and that was a hindrance to information gathering. And sometimes it meant they just didn't get the information they needed and so the records would go unfulfilled.

About an hour into my total demoralization with life as

we knew it, Donovan piped up, "I think I have something."

Blinking thoughts and distractions from my eyes, I turned to him. He was still bent over the book in front of him.

"A ripple went out in 1714 in a small village in Massachusetts. The town itself doesn't even exist anymore, having been absorbed into another. Anyways, a summoner in the area felt it and tracked it down to the hanging execution of a seventeen-year-old girl named Lizzy Maynard."

The news sent a chill through my spine. "What did she do?" I asked, but the gravity of this struck me. He had said that the demon soul merged with the human one when the human body died. If the ripple happened when the girl died, it meant a *child* had sold her soul.

He was quiet for a moment, reading, before he said, "The girl's fourteen-year-old sister had gone missing. They thought the girl was dead, though they had no idea how it may have happened. Weeks after she vanished, someone happened upon her in the woods, tied up and having been experimented on." He paused. "The summoner noted she couldn't get any details about this, because the village folk refused to talk about such 'unholy things,' but she gathered it was grisly.

"She, the summoner, did find one person willing to tell her something. A teenage boy said he'd seen the sister's body, and she'd been badly scarred. He even sketched a picture..." He turned the page and a yellow, wrinkled piece of parchment looked at me with a crudely drawn face half-covered in vine-like scars.

My stomach spun around and tried to vault up my throat. "Well, don't that look damned familiar," I said, barely breathing.

Donovan didn't reply. "The sister lived and told them it had been Lizzy that had done it, though she was 'queer' in herself. Outraged, the townsfolk hung Lizzy and buried her outside of town. The summoner went to the grave and could sense the magical residue of a demonic ritual. She couldn't tell much from it, but there was enough to know such a ritual had happened."

"This has to be the one, right?" I asked softly.

He shrugged. "It certainly seems so," he said. "The summoner never got the chance to meet the victim but saw her at a distance. She described the girl as 'slight of build, with long pale hair and light eyes,' and confirmed the accuracy of the drawing in relation to the scarring."

I nodded slowly. "This has got to be it," I said. "The demon and the girl it took over did to her sister precisely what was done to these girls."

Precisely what was done to me.

"And the girls were killed by hanging, like Lizzy Maynard. The sister was the same build and coloring as these girls."

The same build and coloring as me.

"You said they leave unique scars, like a signature. The scars on the sister are the same as on our victims."

The same scars as on me.

"The problem is, how does that help us find this killer?" I concluded, although it was really just thinking out loud. I knew Donovan couldn't tell me.

He said as much. "I can't tell you that." He smiled apologetically. "I can tell you that when you find this guy, make sure you don't kill him. The essences will merge and make for a more powerful demon. If you take him alive, there's a chance we can gather a circle of summoners that will be able to pull the demon out of the human body while leaving the human's soul—such as it is after making a deal with a demon like that—in the body. It doesn't make up for the crime committed, but at least it keeps the demon from getting any stronger and from being free to be summoned again."

I nodded again, thinking about the cops that had shot

my abductor. They had no idea when they killed Master that they were releasing his black soul to merge with a demon. Who was it that had tortured me all those months, the demon or the man? Why had he called the demon in the first place? What had he wanted so badly? I didn't know, and probably shouldn't even want to know.

"I don't suppose there's any way a summoner can track a demon, like some kind of paranormal bloodhound?" I asked it with a weak smile, but there was a sliver of hope.

He gave me another apologetic smile and shook his head. "I'm afraid not, but these demons work a lot like humans, because they are the remnants of humans. Like serial killers, their patterns are important and they'll repeat them. But they will also get over-confident and maybe even sooner than the average human. Demons are often arrogant by nature. It's kind of a stereotype in fiction these days, but that's because it's true. That means he'll start leaving you enough breadcrumbs to find him, and I'm betting soon. I'll keep looking into this and see if there's anything more that will be useful."

Driving home again, I thought this had been one of the most useful and useless meetings to date.

Chapter Twenty-Three

It was pretty late by the time I got back to the office. Everyone was still there, but they looked like they were on the verge of going home. Vance looked twitchy, and I got the impression he was late for a date with Sadie. I did my best to make it quick and tell them what I'd learned while in the summoner archives.

"Fascinating," Kai said reflectively. "We see patterns repeat in human actions, thoughts and feelings driving them to a compulsion to relive the same experiences over and over again, but I had never heard of a case of this being seen in a demon. Yet this demon seems, we assume from the facts we have, to pursue the same actions every time it takes a new host. So I doubt the actions in regards to kidnapping and torturing teenaged girls stems from any impulse of the current host, though they are a willing accomplice."

"It makes you wonder what they're getting for their part of the deal. What is so important to them that they'd give up their soul to such terrible acts to get it?" Jackson said.

That was pretty much what I had been thinking, but instead of saying so, I just nodded.

"It's late," Vance said. "Let's all get some rest and come at it again tomorrow."

No one was averse to this idea. There was a girl out there who needed us, but we'd be no use to her starved and exhausted. Plus, we didn't know if she was dead or alive... I tried not to think about it. We all needed to recuperate just a little before going at it again, I knew that.

Vance, not surprisingly, was the first one out the door, but Agent Kai wasn't far behind. I lingered to take care of a couple of things at my desk, and Jackson lingered around me.

"Was wondering if you'd let me treat you to a late, late on-the-go dinner to make up for last night," he said.

I glanced up at him in surprise and laughed a little. "Sure, I guess that would be okay. I don't need to get home for my sister tonight." I paused and then felt compelled to explain, "She's staying overnight with my neighbor."

He nodded. "It's nice you have someone so close who can help."

"You don't have to tell me twice," I said, stacking some folders in the corner of my desk and getting to my feet. "And I'm pretty hungry, so food sounds good."

Part of me almost made a joke about it being a date, but that just made me feel weird, so I kept it to myself. We drove separately to Molly's Diner, which was full of the paranormal at that hour, I was sure. Obviously, I didn't have any problem with that, not in this town, but it always made me feel a little bit on the outside. Still, the food was good and fast.

We sat down to eat and talked mostly about the case when we weren't just off in our own worlds, undoubtedly thinking about the case. I knew I was, and it made me a lousy conversationalist. Not that I was a good one to begin with, so it just made me worse, and that was pretty bad.

After that, I went home. It was strange to have the house be so quiet so often, lacking the presence of my sister, but it was for the best. I fed Bunnicula and then threw myself into bed, not bothering to get under the covers or take my clothes off. My one concession was toeing off my shoes, but those were just left cock-eyed near the corner of the bed.

I dreamed of a noose around my neck and four accusing, scarred faces staring at me as I dangled, helpless.

☾ O ☽

The following morning was awful. I woke up feeling like I hadn't slept at all. I got Ana from next door so we could eat breakfast together. A little food and a lot of coffee kept me from being a sleepwalker as I dropped her off at work. I went back home and got some house cleaning done that I'd let lapse, which included fixing a leaky faucet. It was the pleasure of owning one's own home, but I found it to be a grounding experience, and I needed that. If I wasn't careful, I'd get lost. But I didn't linger at home too long, feeling a clock ticking in the back of my mind, so after a shower and change of clothes, I was at the office.

Vance was already there, although our federal buddies were nowhere in sight, and he had only just arrived himself. We walked into the squad room together and found Andrea Sullivan leaning up against my desk.

I paused and counted to four in my head. "Get your ass off my desk."

She arched a dark brow. "It's nice to see you too, Detective." The reporter smirked and didn't get her ass off my desk. "I've actually got something for you, so I think you should be nicer to me."

Vance and I exchanged a look that said neither of us were that keen to do that, but we didn't say so. "What is it, Andy?" he asked.

She reached behind her and picked up a stack of paper held together with a giant binder clip. "I was sent this from the editor of a publishing house who happens to watch the news. She saw Clancy's press conference and heard the other news about what happened to those girls, including a story I wrote. Seeing I was local, she contacted me."

"With what?" I frowned, wondering what the hell this

was about. "If it's something about the case, why call you and not the police?"

Andy's expression was a dry one. "Some people just don't like cops."

I returned the expression. "Even more don't like reporters."

Not one to hold a good retort against a person, she laughed. "True enough, but apparently, this woman wasn't the latter. Though she didn't want to give me a name, and she sounded kind of...embarrassed." She handed the papers to me. The top sheet read *Blood Writ by J. Lanie*. "She just got it a few weeks ago, got around to reading it, and the first chapters sounded too familiar."

I felt ice slide down my spine as I took another look at the book in my hands. It had to be some kind of coincidence, right?

"There's the author's information on the second page," Andy said, finally pushing away from the desk, but I barely noticed now. I stared at the thing in my hands like I was waiting for it to bite me. "The editor said they've published one other work from this author, but it was nothing like this. She said this was far more detailed and gruesome. And the other book didn't spark any news stories. She gave it to me, and now I'm making it your problem."

Vance watched her as she started to leave. "When will the news story be out?"

She stopped and looked back with a wry smile. "I'm not always the cold heart, you know. This time around, I want the guy caught more than I want the story. I hope it helps." And with that, Andy walked out.

I slowly sat at my desk and set the book in front of me. Vance dragged a chair beside me. "Do you really think this could be from the killer?" he asked. He looked about as wary of it as I was. If this was from the killer, if the fuck was sick enough to write about what was done to those girls, the poison and evil might be in the pages. Could a demon possess something inanimate?

While we stared at the book like it was a rattlesnake, Jackson and Kai came in, and Vance got them up to date.

"Are you just going to stare at it?" Jackson asked.

"I was thinking about it," I said, finally tearing my gaze away to look at him. I don't know what he saw in my eyes, but it made him blink. That made me blink, and I forced myself to look away.

He reached past me to take it and caught a uniform. "We need three more copies of this made by yesterday. I don't care if you have to handcuff someone to keep them away from the machine to get it done." The uniform, a hire new enough to still have the big eyes, nodded and hurried off.

The appearance of Jackson and Kai seemed to galvanize us to action. Vance said, "I'll see if I can find any information on the author." He went off to snag the top sheet back from the scurrying officer.

I snapped out of my daze when a buried piece of information broke loose in my head. I looked at Jackson and frowned. "Lanie, that sounds familiar. Wasn't that the name of one of the authors Davidson emailed?"

Jackson snapped. "I think you're right. Good catch, Nykk." He turned to Kai. "Go talk to the techs and start digging through the girl's computer again. If they find anything about 'J. Lanie,' have them print it out and bring it here." Kai nodded and hurried off while he sat down in front of me. The energy of having more leads was nearly visible in the squad room, around Jackson and Vance and Kai, but I wasn't sure I felt it.

"Are you okay?" he asked.

I pulled back out of myself enough to look at him. I tried to put the shutters down inside my head, inside my eyes. I didn't need anyone looking in, seeing what I didn't want anyone to see. "Of course," I replied automatically.

He eyed me suspiciously, like he didn't believe me. I suppose I couldn't blame him, but neither of us said anything else.

❨○❩

A couple of hours later found us all reading one thing or another. Jackson and I had set about reading the book while Kai was scouring emails and Vance was glued to his computer, searching for information on the author.

"This writer is a ghost," he finally said, pushing his keyboard away in frustration. "The address is a P.O. Box to a fake ID, and the phone number goes nowhere. The email is a free web server, so they don't have anything either."

"Your local technical gremlin is trying to pull I.P. information off what's on Davidson's computer," Kai said without looking up from her printouts. "There are emails with this J. Lanie, but they are very smart and never say anything useful. There's one comment about flowers outside the window, asters, which match the pollen found on the tape, but that doesn't really do anything for us."

I listened to them with half of my attention. The other half was absorbed in this awful book. That was to say it was an awful topic. The writing really wasn't that bad, and that was part of the problem. The writer really delved into the story. A good story draws you into the character whose head the text is in, but I desperately didn't want to be dragged in.

The door at the top of the stairs shut. It didn't slam, but the sound of wood hitting wood and the metal clicking together still sounded painfully loud to Marie and her body jerked. The basement flooded with darkness, the door stealing the last of the light, leaving her to stare into nothingness and contemplate her existence.

It was hard to figure out what hurt worse, because everything hurt. The ropes tying her to the table burned against her skin. Her struggles had worn her wrists and ankles raw. Her throat felt scorched from her screaming, which had faded now into a pathetic whimper of the question: why me?

"Nykk!"

I snapped out of it and looked away from the book. "What?" Looking between Vance and Jackson, I blinked.

"You just seemed like you were in another zip code," Jackson commented, still looking concerned.

"Just reading," I said. "I'm a pretty focused reader." Truth was, I wasn't at all a focused reader. I didn't sit still to read well enough and got easily distracted. This book, however, was different. The tidal wave of memories swished in the back of my mind, wanting to surge forward and spill over me.

Why me?

"It's not impossible that someone totally unrelated to the case wrote this, but it seems unlikely with the timing of it going to the editor and the details about the scars and injuries, the description of the abduction and captivity." I tried to deflect their attentions with a focus on work. That was why we were there, right?

"That's what I was thinking," Jackson agreed. He hefted the papers briefly. "I wonder how it ends."

CHAPTER TWENTY-FOUR

The hours stretched out. We read the book and worked on other angles, doing all the more tedious elements of our work. I lost track of time, however, because I focused on reading. No one bothered me, or if they tried, I didn't notice and they didn't try very hard.

By the time the night got late and rolled past midnight, we hadn't been able to accomplish much. But my brain was on fire. Images from the book tugged at memories and memories sunk into the pages and stirred them up. Every scar I had from those eleven months seared like they were new again. Phantom pain inside my body reminded me of broken bones, fractures, poisons, contusions, and lacerations. The terms I had learned in my adult life melded with the feelings of the past.

I was vaguely aware of Kai leaving to do something and Vance going out for food and some air while Jackson took a nap in the break room. No one wanted to leave for good when it felt like we had our first real lead that could *lead us to something*. A dull buzz of activity remained elsewhere in the station, but I blocked it out. I was alone with the book and what it did to me, but amidst the torment, I felt streaks of clarity. Details stood out.

"I love the flowers that bloom in autumn," I whispered to myself, plucking the vague string of words from the depths of my mind. It had been something Master had said to me once, though I little remarked it at the time. At the time, I'd been a little distracted, but I never really forgot anything of my time there. Some things stood out more than others, but pain makes everything important and clear.

There was pollen of asters on the tape and Master loved autumn-blooming flowers, like the New England aster... The girl had been in Massachusetts when she summoned the demon and let it take her, and it had been in autumn. Crystal Davidson had screamed something about flowers. Pieces dropped and clicked, and I couldn't escape that there had been a demon whispering in Master's ear the same way the demon now whispered in the ear of the woman killing these girls.

Mary Ellen James, gone missing in July. That meant she had been in the killer's grasp for four months. That was seven months less than eleven. She hadn't been found yet. There'd been no more bodies dumped off the freeway. She was still alive.

Master kept me in a basement. I never left the basement. A dim window lit from above, but it was dirty and I could never see through it or get a clear stream of sunlight, so it was always dark. Nearly a year in darkness, but by four months it had been bad enough.

My limbs felt stiff and achy as I flipped through the manuscript pages again. The killer in the book kept his—it was a man—captives in the basement. Why was it always basements, cold and dark? Mary Ellen was probably looking for a window. Crystal said she cried a lot. Had I cried? I was certain I had, but I didn't like to think about it. I put the book down and grabbed the stack of printed emails from Crystal's computer. J. Lanie talked about flowers. What was with the damn flowers?

Turning in my chair, I looked at the board. Five faces stared down at me. I looked back at them for a time. At the end was Mary Ellen, only she was smiling. Her photo wasn't the ashen, scarred complexion of a corpse.

I looked at the map. There were pins and lines marking where girls had been taken and where they had been dropped. The bookstore Mary Ellen had last been seen in was on the map. She had been in the mysteries and thrillers section. Maybe she had been looking at the book by J. Lanie or knew of her. I moved my gaze to the center of the map, where I had outlined the possible 'hot zone' with my inelegant estimate. I wasn't an expert in geographic profiling, but it was a good start.

I had to think like the killer. I had to think like Master. If I wanted to keep a bunch of girls and do terrible things to them, I wouldn't want anyone to know. I wouldn't want them found in my house. Maybe an abandoned house, or one empty for a long time, like the killer in the book. Cops didn't usually think along those lines, because most people stick close to their own homes...but this wasn't most people.

Houses on the market, I thought. The housing market still wasn't great, and a lot of places had sat unoccupied for more than a year. What about one of those houses?

My mind raced. I rushed to my computer and started pulling up real estate listings for the area I had marked as the hot zone. I looked for houses with basements, because they would be in the basement. I looked for houses with garages, because there was a car and automotive oil. The killer wouldn't want anyone seeing his car, right?

Her car...

The house had to be on the market for a year or more, because that made it unlikely to have people going through it too often. It was still a calculated risk, but the killer could escape and just leave the grisly discovery and never be known.

I couldn't let that happen. We had to catch her. We had to find Mary Ellen.

My search narrowed down, and I looked through them. There were a little less than a dozen, but one picture screamed at me. There were flowers lining the garage and the house. I didn't know what they were, if it was the right kind of flowers, but it caught me all the same. Something in my head screamed, "*This is the one!*"

My heart started pounding so hard it made it difficult to breathe. I pictured Mary Ellen tied up in that basement, crying and screaming and burned and scarred.

I had to save her.

Grabbing my stuff, I rushed out of the squad room. There was no one there to see me, and no one asked me where I was going. I got into my car and took off for the address, blinded with the need to find that girl. She had to be spared one more moment of terror and agony.

The drive wasn't a long one, but it afforded me enough time for my blood to start to cool a little.

I pulled up across the street from the house and cut the engine. Immediately, the autumn chill seeped into my car. Had I even turned the heat on in the first place? It didn't matter. I stared at the house through the gray pre-dawn light, and every muscle tensed as I contemplated going in. What would I find?

On impulse, I grabbed my phone and dialed Vance's number, subject to a brief moment of uncertainty.

It rang several times, and then the voicemail answered.

"Vance, it's me. I think I was calling to have you talk me out of this, but since you didn't answer, I guess that means I should do it." I turned it off and dropped the phone in the center console, never taking my eyes off the house.

Finally, I got out of the car. I pulled my gun from my shoulder holster and moved in.

The house was dark, both inside and out. The night was unusually silent, and I thought that everyone in the neighborhood would hear my beating heart. Checking to all sides every few moments, I saw no one around, and no one was watching as I came around to the back door. I found it was unlocked, so I held the gun low while I slowly twisted the handle and slipped inside as quietly as I could.

The light from the moon was as much as I could see by, but I could make out that I was in a small room with a washer and dryer. I frowned, at first thinking that rooms like this were the most likely to have crap to trip on, but then I reminded myself this was a house for sale. No one lived here...

No one but the killer...and Mary Ellen.

I crept through the room and entered a short hall. On the other side, I thought I saw a refrigerator and then just to the left of that, a dim light crept around the edge of door. It flickered like firelight, and I took a deep breath. There was someone down there, and I knew who it was.

With my eyes glued to that flicker of light, I stalked forward. I tried to keep low, but every nerve felt like it had electricity in it.

As I got nearer, I thought I heard a faint whimpering and a low murmur. I had to stop as a rush of dizziness washed over me. I remembered making that noise, and I remembered listening to that voice. The muscles of my arms trembled, and my body tried to lie down.

Be a good girl and just lay still, just like that, oh, you're such a good girl.

I forced myself to stay standing and then I forced myself to keep walking. I reached the door and stopped breathing for a long moment, hooking the door with my toe and lifting my gun. I walked down the stairs slowly and moved past the rafter blocking my view, seeing the small, stocky body and short, dark hair of the person bending over the table with the girl tied to it.

The second-to-last step creaked. The girl cried out. The woman whirled around, but then the face smiled. I didn't know the face, but I knew the voice.

"I never thought I'd see *you* again."

CHAPTER TWENTY-FIVE

"Help me! Help me, please!"

Mary Ellen wailed from behind the woman, who turned her head back and quietly said, "Hush now."

With a faint mewling noise, the girl bit her lip and shrunk back.

That's a good girl now.

The woman turned back to me and smiled again. "It's so good to see you, but you know it's not right to hold a gun on your master."

My eyes flickered down, and I realized I had lifted the gun higher, had it trained on the woman's head. My arms twitched, trying to lower, to obey, but my higher mind stopped it.

"You're not my master," I said softly, but with less conviction than I meant.

Chuckling, the demon shook her head. "You always were a stubborn thing. It took so long to get you to obey properly, but once you did, you were the best girl I ever had." She started to walk around the table.

I opened my mouth to tell her not to move, but I said nothing. She'd turned her back on me. Now was my chance to shoot her and end this.

Master trusted me, because I was a good girl.

How dare she turn her back on me!

Save Mary Ellen...

By now, the demon was on the other side of the table and once again had turned to face me. "This little one broke easily, which suited my tasks but wasn't as much fun as the ones who tested my skills." The smile was chilling. It chilled me. I remembered damp, cold basements. "You don't really want to shoot me."

Again, I trembled. I fought with my arms to keep the gun steady.

"You deserve to die," I said, my voice still straining to rise above a whisper. "For what you've done to those girls. For what you did to me. For what you did to your sister. Lizzy."

The smile faded, and fire flashed through her eyes. Almost real fire. A flashing of red-orange through otherwise dark eyes. "You always were such a *clever girl*," she sneered, but then caught herself and forced a smile. This time, I could see it was forced. A crack appeared in the ice around me.

My eyes dropped to the girl on the table. Her eyes met mine and I saw the bruises on her cheeks and the bags under her eyes, but she wasn't scarred yet. Blonde and thin and so young... Scarred, but unscarred.

Her gaze pleaded with me to save her.

I felt my finger shiver on the trigger, but I couldn't do it.

"Put that gun away, Nykk." The demon's tone of command was unmistakable and familiar. It coursed through me, straight through to the fourteen-year-old girl trapped in the depths of my brain. She cried and curled up, but I didn't.

Stay still. It will only hurt for a moment.

Fire flashed through my scars, and I winced. The demon smiled.

Why are you hurting me?

She deserved to die. She deserved to hang, again, but I wasn't empowered to do that. But I was empowered...to do this. I had the gun.

Please, release me.

My finger twitched again, but then I heard a voice behind me.

"Nykk, don't."

A voice from my past, but he's never been in the basement with me before, what is he doing here?

Jackson.

Blinking away images, past and present, I didn't turn away. I kept the gun trained on the demon, because she deserved to die! She'd hurt me! She's hurting me!

Wait…

"Nykk," the voice said again. His tone was measured and calm, comforting and strong. "Put the gun down. We're here to take care of you."

I slowly started to lower the gun, and people flooded around me like a river crashing around a rock. They grabbed the demon, who looked too shocked to offer any resistance as they did so, but then the look turned angry. Posey Kai and another female officer rushed in and got Mary Ellen off the table, supporting her between them as they moved up the stairs. The poor thing sobbed and thanked them, over and over.

Jackson had his hand on my wrist, pushing the gun toward the floor.

"You've disappointed me," the demon said.

Tears lined my eyes, but I couldn't look away.

"Donovan is here, and he's got the summoner cavalry," Jackson said, speaking in the same tone, like that of a man trying to stop someone from jumping off a ledge. "He's learned more about the demon, and they're going to take care of it."

The demon's eyes widened suddenly with something I'd never seen: fear. It made something go cold in my stomach. *I'd never seen Master afraid.* She suddenly started struggling against the people holding her, thrashing desperately, but they held her firm. Her face contorted with terror and rage. The heavyset cops holding the small female body didn't seem concerned. Both had strange markings written in white paint on the backs of their hands. The cop inside me guessed it was summoner protection against the demon's magic, and it seemed to work.

Somewhere in the back of my mind, a fourteen-year-old girl was screaming in protest and exultation, in concern and pitiful relief. I heard and felt her, and yet observed that girl from a distance, as we both watched what unfolded.

Donovan came down the stairs with three strangers behind him. As he walked past me, he offered a weak smile. Did I look crazy? I must have looked crazy. I watched in horror and fascination as they walked right up to the demon in the human's body, struggling against the cops holding her.

"It has to be done here," Jackson said. I realized his arm was around my shoulder, warm but not burning.

Donovan drew a chalk circle around the demon, adding symbols to the cold cement, and then other things I didn't recognize. The others did more, and none seemed too concerned. Power in numbers. My consciousness seemed to weave in and out. The human body screamed as the four surrounded it and chanted, magic making even my human skin tingle. The demon nearly wrestled itself from the grip of the cops in its final desperate attempt to escape before the violent spasms and terrible screams that seemed to last forever, then the body sunk down. Donovan held a box in his hands that I hadn't noticed before. Wooden and old, with a wrought iron latch engraved with more strange symbols.

"Is it gone?" I whispered as he passed me.

"You're safe now," he said with another self-conscious smile, walking up the stairs with his comrades silently in tow.

☾O☽

Sitting outside on the cold lawn in the pre-dawn air, I stared at flashing cop lights and leaned against Jackson.

"We saw the search window open on your computer and came here. It wasn't really that hard," he explained. "We tried to call you on the way, and when we didn't get an answer, well..."

I laughed weakly as the human body was led, half-carried, to a cop car. "What will happen to her?"

He shrugged. "She'll be charged. Will probably try to plead mitigation for the demon's control, but she invited it in. I doubt it will hold."

"It always holds," I whispered.

Chapter Twenty-Six

"**C**an you tell me about it?"

I had my feet curled up on the couch and my arms around my knees, a 0.5mg dose of the popular tranquilizer Xanax coursing through my blood, as I sat on the psychiatrist's couch for my mandated appointment. I would have come even if they hadn't told me I had to. I'd be calling Dr. Kohl more too.

Sighing, I replied, "Her name is Janet Meyers, and she's thirty-seven. Only has an associate's degree from a community college, but it was in criminal justice, and she'd taken forensics courses. It helped her to hide the crimes... and herself."

She nodded but didn't say anything. It was a psychological trick to get me to keep talking, and it worked.

"They found so much evidence in the house and garage, on top of having the girl tied up in the basement when they got there, that there's no way she can try to get out of it. Jackson was right in that she's trying to plead mitigation, but they're lining up Donovan and another summoner to testify she had to purposely summon the demon. They think—" I laughed morbidly. "It looks like she wanted the demon to help her write a book that would be realistic and make her rich. She let this monster back into the world to kill four girls and devastate a fifth to write a fucking book and make money. Maybe she didn't want to go that far, but she set it loose and let it do its bidding through her."

Sighing again, I looked out the window and saw Adelheid in the distance. I went on dully, "People will be talking about why she did it. Most won't want to believe it was this simple. A woman calling a demon and killing four people to write a book? I don't know. Maybe there was more in her background that fucked her up. But you know? I don't care."

"Why is that?" Such little questions for such big concepts.

"I got fucked up early on and haven't killed anyone."

The morning before going to the counselor, I had finally looked at my own case file. And it was surprisingly useless. They knew almost nothing of the man who did this to me, except his name was Harold. I kind of wished I hadn't looked.

Now I was on suspension from my job because of my "cowboy" move. I didn't blame Captain Roy. It was the right call, because I had let it get to me. I could see it very clearly in hindsight. I had lost all objectivity and did something really, really *stupid*.

"What happens now?" the psychiatrist prompted after a moment. I was a little surprised she hadn't pushed on my last statement, but maybe she sensed I wanted to move on.

"Now?" I laughed softly. "I hope Janet Meyers gets locked away for a long time." I paused and looked at my hands. "And I'm resigning from the force." I bit my lip. "I don't think I can do it anymore, even if they'd give me the job back. I don't know if they will, but it doesn't matter."

"What will you do instead?"

This brought the first real smile to my lips, even if it was a tiny one. "I'm going to become a victim's advocate." I lifted my eyes and met hers, straight on. "I think I could be pretty good at it, because I know where they're coming from. I know what it's like to be a victim."

Later that afternoon, I did it.

I went to the station to hand in my resignation to Captain Roy, and I cleaned out my desk. I realized, as I put stuff into the cardboard box, that there was very little of mine here in the office. Briefly, I wondered if I'd made any kind of mark, or any kind of difference, while I'd been here.

Glancing up, I realized Vance was watching me. Arms folded across his chest, he leaned back against the desk and had a curious look in his amber eyes.

"Are you sure about this?" he asked. "I'm sure they wouldn't fire you. Give you shit for a while, you were a dumbass, but you'd still have your job."

I smiled a little. "Yeah, I'm sure. I just can't anymore. I need a change."

He didn't look like he liked it, but he accepted it. That was as much as I needed to know. "So, what now?"

"Sullivan thinks I should write a book," I said with a dark half-smile.

He cocked a brow. "But seriously, folks?"

I chuckled faintly. "I'm going to be a victim's advocate." He nodded. "I'm also going to track down my brother. It's time that I really made an effort to make us a family again." I'd decided that after my therapist's appointment.

He tilted his head to one side and then chuckled. "Talk to Dakota. She can find anyone."

I snorted, thinking about the *very* grumpy hardass hunter at the Stanton Agency with the affinity for animal forms with sharp teeth. "I don't know if I'm *that* mad at the guy."

I finished putting my stuff in the box and then walked over to him. I wasn't good at this stuff, but I felt compelled.

Yet even as I stood before him, I didn't know what to do or say. I uncomfortably rolled my shoulders, looking at the tops of my sneakers.

Taking the initiative, he grabbed me and hugged me tight. I froze instinctively but forced myself to loosen up and return the embrace. I put my head briefly against his shoulder, letting myself take comfort in the human (generically speaking) contact and what it meant.

I stepped back a moment later and smiled a little. "Hope this doesn't mean we won't still see each other sometimes. I'd like to stay friends."

"You got it, kid." He grinned. I'd say it was almost wolfish, but it didn't seem right to say a weretiger had a wolfish look.

Before either of us could get any more uncomfortable with the bonding moment, Jackson came in.

Vance looked up in surprise.

"My ride," I explained. Ana was with him.

Ana came up and hugged me without saying anything, and I hugged her back. It was easier with her. Jackson nodded a classic Male Greeting with Vance and waited until we'd separated to smile at me. "How're you doing?" he asked the million-dollar question.

I waved good-bye to Vance, grabbed my box, and we started walking out of the building. I considered the question. "I'm…okay," I replied honestly, letting myself sink a little more from the demeanor I'd kept up with Vance. "I'm as okay as I can be right now. It's going to take a while, though."

He nodded. I knew he wanted to say he understood but couldn't say it because he couldn't do it. There were few who could.

"Any word on how Mary Ellen is doing?" I asked after a moment. I should have asked Vance, but I'd gotten distracted.

"Posey says she's doing all right," he replied. "She's out of the hospital and back home, already starting her own trips to the therapist." We reached the car, and he opened the back door politely for Ana, then took my box to set it on the seat beside her before walking around with me to the front passenger's side door of his black sedan.

Before he could open my door, I stopped him with a weak smile. "I just wanted to say thanks, you know, for being here during all of this. You've been...a friend, when I needed one, and I appreciate it."

His smile wasn't as weak as mine as he rested a hand on my arm. "Of course," he said, "and don't think it'll stop here. I already lost track of you once. I don't plan to let it happen again."

My smile grew a little as I got in the car. Yeah, I wasn't planning to lose me anymore either.

POSTLUDE

"*E*verything had changed."

"*What had changed?*" you ask.

She paces behind the chair, holding her arms tightly around her body. "*My dad died of a heart attack. My mom is a mess. Peter is okay, but Ana isn't doing well.*" Slowly, she shakes her head. "*My family has fallen apart, and it is all my fault!*"

"*It isn't your fault, Nykk.*"

"*That's what they keep saying,*" she mutters darkly. "*But my family was good and healthy and happy before I was taken. Now, it's fallen apart. Peter doesn't seem to know what to do with me. My mom can't look at me without crying. She says it's because she's happy, but I worry that seeing me is a reminder of how everything is fucked up.*" She pauses and looks at you. "*Sorry.*"

"*It's all right,*" you reply indulgently. "*Just go on.*"

Coming to a stop, she puts her hands on the back of the chair. "*Ana hasn't gotten to as many of her classes and such. She has these emotional outbursts. She already has enough to worry about. My mom, too. They don't need more trouble, but I can barely handle myself. How am I supposed to help? But I'm the oldest! It's my job to help!*" She starts pacing again. "*I'm supposed to help. I'm supposed to be good, right, be on top of things. Not...trouble.*"

You give her a few moments while she visibly pulls herself back together, even though she seems to retreat back into her *shell.*

"You don't know what it's like," she whispers, "to have your own mother look at you and have her eyes fill with pain. I don't think she blames me, exactly, but she can't stop thinking about the bad things when she sees my face." She finally sits back down and sighs. "I can't talk to her about this. I can't talk to anyone about this. I guess you're the only person I can. I don't want anyone else to know. No one can understand."

Lifting her face, she meets your gaze and holds it now. Fear fills hers. "You won't tell anyone what I said, right?"

Author's Note

It's me again!

As I write this, it's mid-October. I'm skating in under the wire to get this uploaded in time for the preorder, but things have been busy and crazy. The world is still going through all sorts of insanity, and we're all just holding on the best we can.

At least I can be happy that it's autumn in New England, which is such a beautiful time! It's my favorite season, hands down. Summer is way too hot, but autumn is pretty perfect. My dog likes it too, although he's very fluffy and likes the winter and snow the best.

Anyways, here we are. Book four.

This one was a tough one to write. I was bound and determined to get the police procedural aspect as accurate as I could, make sure all the hints and clues lined up, and also do justice to the character: a broken woman doing the best to make the most of an unbroken life.

The interludes were actually written separately from the book, then broken into pieces and spaced throughout to give you a view into Nykk's psyche and her past while we move along with her future. Even if it's not an 'easy' story, though, I hope you appreciated reading along with Nykk's journey.

If you want to know more about the town of Adelheid, the people who live in it, and the lore I chose to use when writing these preternatural species, you can check out my series wiki at wiki.authorkbthorne.com.

Sincerely,

K. B. Thorne, October 2020

ABOUT THE AUTHOR

Born a Connecticut Yankee in nobody's court, K. B. Thorne grew up to brave snow and talk fast.

She started reading when she was three and never looked back, soon frequently falling asleep with a book under her cheek. At eleven, she discovered *Night Mare* by Piers Anthony and entered the world of grown-up fantasy fiction. As you can guess, it was all over from there. She started writing at fourteen, then met vampires as a teenager and the concept for what would become Adelheid (now the Blood Rights Series) was soon born. Mia Darien followed a few years later, and the books were released.

However, K. B. is also a third-generation Trekkie. Somewhere in a vault at Paramount is a very angry letter written by her grandmother when *Star Trek: The Original Series* was cancelled, so sci-fi is in the blood too. Alongside a love of love and an adoration for her first love of epic fantasy.

K. B. Thorne is the evolution of Mia Darien after years of learning and living. She has taken both of those things to become a smarter, better writer with a fresh new face and take on the literary world. Thorne writes the urban fantasy, fantasy and sci-fi, while Sadie Johnston writes the romance.

These days, when she's not desperately trying to find time to write, she works as a freelance editor/cover artist/formatter and happily lives her unconventional life alongside her very own Named Man of the North and their mini-tank. (Who is, you know, their son.)

You can find K. B. at authorkbthorne.com!

OTHER BOOKS BY K. B. THORNE

Writing as K. B. Thorne
Blood Rights Series

Bad Blood
Blood and Thunder
Blood Moon
Written in Blood
Bloodshot
First Blood
Out for Blood
New Blood
Flesh and Blood

Out for Blood Series
Bones & Blood

Bellator (Anthology)
Good Things (Anthology)
Ashes to Sunrise (Anthology)
The Shape of Tomorrow (Anthology)
Born of Defiance (Anthology)

Writing as Sadie Johnston (Romance)
Beauty
Help Wanted (with Viola Dawn)
Threnody (with Alastair Malone)
Here, Kitty Kitty (Anthology)
Amor Vincit Omnia (Anthology)
Second Chances (Anthology)